U0119617

全民英檢學習指南
中高級聽讀測驗

The Official Preparation Guide to the GEPT

High-Intermediate Level Test

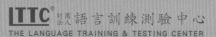

財團法人語言訓練測驗中心
THE LANGUAGE TRAINING & TESTING CENTER

前言

　　「全民英檢」（GEPT）分級標準參考我國學制與教育部英語課程綱要，題型與命題內容符合各階段英語學習者的特質與需要。GEPT 自 2000 年推出至今，持續進行信效度研究，精進測驗品質。自 2021 年 1 月起，GEPT 調整初、中、中高級聽讀測驗的題型與內容，並提供成績回饋服務，另，旨在反映 108 國教新課綱以「素養」為核心的教育理念與「學習導向評量（Learning Oriented Assessment）」的精神，期透過適當的測驗內容與成績回饋，更有效地促進學習，提升國人英語溝通力。

　　題型調整後，GEPT 內容將更貼近日常生活，且更符合我國各階段英語學習的歷程，例如：納入更多元的體裁和文本，評量真實生活、校園與職場情境下英語溝通及解決問題的能力。

　　為幫助學習者熟悉題型調整後 GEPT 的測驗內容與題型，降低實際測驗時的焦慮感，並培養正確的英語學習方法與策略，本中心特別編製《全民英檢學習指南》系列。有別於市面上著重於應試技巧的測驗準備書籍，本書以學習為導向，並融入培養核心素養的學習建議，期盼學習者除了持續累積英語實力外，亦能培養統整歸納與反思評鑑等關鍵思辯能力。

　　本中心期許《全民英檢學習指南》能正向強化讀者的學習動機，培養積極的學習態度。不論是準備全民英檢的學習者，報考會考、指考、學測的學生或是希望加強英語能力的自學者，皆可藉本書的試題檢視自己聽解與閱讀能力的強弱項，並配合書中的學習建議持續練習，我們相信學習者定能精進英語實力。

執行長　沈冬

財團法人語言訓練測驗中心

3

CONTENTS

全民英檢學習指南—中高級聽讀測驗

目次　　　前言 ………… 3

導讀 ………… 6

中高級聽力與閱讀測驗簡介 ………… 8

練習題

聽力測驗 ………… 13

閱讀測驗 ………… 21

聽力與閱讀測驗解答 ……… 38

聽力測驗錄音內容 ………… 40

學習指南

聽力測驗

第一部份：問答 ………… 55

第二部份：對話 ………… 73

第三部份：談話 ………… 105

閱讀測驗

第一部份：詞彙 ………… 133

第二部份：段落填空 …… 153

第三部份：閱讀理解 …… 175

導讀

　　本書是專為英語程度 CEFR B2 學習者設計的學習指南，可以做為準備全民英檢中高級使用，也適合自修、練習使用。本書分兩部份，第一部份為聽力閱讀練習題，第二部份為學習指南。練習題依照全民英檢正式測驗規格編寫，難易度、長度等都與正式測驗相同，測驗的設計以學習為導向，並融入核心素養，鼓勵自主學習，幫助學習者強化英文實力。學習指南內容包括：

1. 題型說明：簡介題型與評量的能力

2. 考前提醒：提示評量重點、題型與應答要訣

3. 試題解析：詳解題目與選項；2021 年起調整的題型以 `New!` 標記

4. 關鍵字詞：提供關鍵字釋義、例句與延伸學習

5. 學習策略：加強聽解、閱讀能力與相關核心素養的學習方法與策略

針對閱讀理解題的長篇文章，進一步提供：

6. 文本分析：解析文章的架構，說明每段的主旨與內容

7. 延伸思考：深化對文章主題的理解，提供延伸思考題，鍛鍊系統性思考與
　　　　　　　解決問題的核心素養

使用說明

步驟一 練習限時作答聽力閱讀練習題。

　　√ 請搭配隨附 MP3 光碟或掃描 QR code 聆聽聽力音檔，並依照規定
　　　的作答時間作答。

　　√ 作答完畢後，請核對答案。

　　√ 檢視自己答錯的題目，聽力部份可對照錄音稿確認自己沒聽懂的關
　　　鍵訊息，閱讀部份則再仔細閱讀一次文本。

步驟二 研讀學習指南。

　　√ 先看題型說明與考前提醒，了解各題型可運用的策略與注意事項，
　　　想想看有哪些策略是自己忽略的，並練習運用在答題。

　　√ 閱讀試題解析，特別留意自己答錯的題目需運用的能力，再加強自
　　　己的弱項。

　　√ 閱讀文本分析，了解長篇文章的架構與脈絡，幫助進一步理解文章
　　　內容。

　　√ 閱讀關鍵字詞，透過所提供的例句，學習如何靈活運用相關詞彙。

　　√ 查閱延伸思考，透過本書提供的思考問題加深對該議題的理解，並
　　　培養批判性思考。

　　√ 最後讀學習策略所提供的建議，持續累積實力。

中高級聽力與閱讀測驗簡介

	中高級 聽力測驗					中高級 閱讀測驗			
時間	部份	題型	題數	總題數	時間	部份	題型	題數	總題數
約 35 分鐘	一	問答	10	40	50 分鐘	一	詞彙	10	40
	二	對話	15			二	段落填空	10	
	三	談話	15			三	閱讀理解	20	

能力說明

英語能力逐漸成熟，應用領域擴大，雖有錯誤，但無礙溝通。

聽力

能聽懂日常生活與工作場合中較長的對話，並能聽懂電話留言、廣告、新聞報導等內容較長的談話，以及工作場合的簡報、演講、討論、產品介紹及操作說明等。

通過中高級的英語學習者能夠輕鬆地辨識語音、迅速掌握詞句語意，能從範圍較廣的上下文脈絡理解言談。能聽懂母語人士在正常語速下進行內容較長、訊息較複雜的對話和談話，並掌握主旨大意、細節、目的、說話者的態度、意見、立場、關係等。能聽懂日常生活中的電話留言、公眾場所廣播，即使主題不熟悉、內容較抽象的電視廣告和新聞報導等，也能大致聽懂。學術與職場上能聽懂內容和語言組織較複雜的演講、工作簡報、業務討論、產品說明與操作注意事項等。

閱讀

能閱讀日常生活中不同體裁的文章及書信、說明書及報章雜誌等，與工作場合的文件、圖表、正式書信與議論文等。

通過中高級的英語學習者能理解日常生活中不同領域、體裁與主題較抽象的長篇文章，且能因應不同的閱讀目的，有效運用適切的閱讀策略理解讀物。能快速掌握文章大意與關鍵細節。能統整歸納多篇文章的訊息，並根據隱含的線索與文章脈絡推論、詮釋作者的立場與觀點。此外，字彙量廣泛且能根據上下文猜測生詞的意義，但理解使用頻率較低的慣用語仍有困難。能迅速擷取篇幅較長與內容較複雜的書信、報章雜誌與說明書等的重點並找出關鍵資訊。學術與職場上能讀懂自身領域相關的專業文章、圖表、議論文等。

通過標準

級數	測驗項目	通過標準
中高級	聽力測驗 閱讀測驗	兩項測驗成績總和達 160 分，且其中任一項成績不低於 72 分。

Note

練習題

全民英語能力分級檢定測驗
GENERAL ENGLISH PROFICIENCY TEST

中高級聽力測驗
HIGH-INTERMEDIATE LISTENING COMPREHENSION TEST

掃描 QR Code
聆聽音檔

This listening comprehension test will test your ability to understand spoken English. In this test, each conversation, talk and question will be spoken JUST ONE TIME. They will not be written out for you. There are three parts to this test. Special instructions will be given to you at the beginning of each part.

Part I: Answering Questions

In Part I, you will hear ten questions. After you hear a question, read the four choices in your test booklet and decide which one is the best answer to the question you have heard.

Example:

You will hear: I heard all flights to Penghu have been delayed due to thick fog at the airport.

You will read: A.   When will the sky there clear up?
                      B.   Is the engine still out of order?
                      C.   How did they lose the luggage?
                      D.   Could it be the only aisle seat?

The best answer to the question "I heard all flights to Penghu have been delayed due to thick fog at the airport." is A: "When will the sky there clear up?" Therefore, you should choose answer A.

Please turn to the next page. ●

1. A. My appointment is next week.
   B. His clinic is very near here.
   C. I went on Monday.
   D. He was in the hospital.

2. A. Could you wait until after class?
   B. You're flattering me.
   C. How on earth did you solve it?
   D. I'm glad that we could work this out.

3. A. I'd love to. Thanks for the offer.
   B. Sure. I missed your great cooking.
   C. My bad. I had to get settled first.
   D. No wonder. It's such a small town.

4. A. At least it'll be good exercise.
   B. That'll be enough, thanks.
   C. Not again. I haven't saved any of them.
   D. They fell down and got hurt.

5. A. Okay. I'll check out volume two.
   B. Sorry. I didn't know it was so loud.
   C. Why not? Wasn't he listening?
   D. Of course. He can come with Louis.

6. A. As soon as possible.
   B. Around the corner.
   C. For one hour.
   D. Very rarely.

7. A. Yes, but she lives in a dormitory.
   B. Yes, and she almost succeeded.
   C. No, but I lost contact with her.
   D. No, and you're not going without her.

8. A. They haven't arrived yet.
   B. When is it effective?
   C. I'm still considering it, though.
   D. The new recruits need training.

9. A. Yes, I'm working on the first draft.
   B. Yes, both of them canceled the meeting.
   C. No, I can't decide which class to take.
   D. No, they're still negotiating some details.

10. A. It's merely a myth.
    B. I couldn't agree more.
    C. A statement will be released.
    D. You'd better check the source.

L   L   L   L   L

Part II: Conversations

In Part II, you will hear several conversations between a man and a woman. After each conversation, you will hear one to two questions about the conversation. After you hear the question, read the four choices in your test booklet and choose the best answer to the question you have heard.

Example:

<u>You will hear</u>:

(Woman)   I want to make a fruit salad for the picnic tomorrow.

(Man)   Okay, how about these bananas?

(Woman)   No, they're too green and too firm.

(Man)   Why don't we buy these dragon fruit? They look ready to eat.

(Woman)   Good, get two of those. The mangos are nice and soft, too; let's grab one.

Question: On what basis are the speakers selecting ingredients?

<u>You will read</u>:

A. How ripe the items are.
B. How their flavors will blend.
C. How expensive each variety is.
D. How long it takes to prepare them.

The best answer to the question "On what basis are the speakers selecting ingredients?" is A: "How ripe the items are." Therefore, you should choose answer A.

L   L   L   L   L

11. A. A beginner.
    B. A portrait specialist.
    C. An experienced amateur.
    D. A professional.

12. A. Study for a final exam.
    B. Visit friends in the dormitory.
    C. Work on an important paper.
    D. Attend an economics class.

13. A. Following a large animal's footprints.
    B. Observing a creature from a distance.
    C. Making a quick sketch in the wild.
    D. Chasing a rare insect in the woods.

14. A. He's leaving on Friday.
    B. He needs to revise it.
    C. He asked for it last week.
    D. He'll be gone next week.

15. A. Because of unpleasant surroundings.
    B. Because of a new road.
    C. Because of a strict law.
    D. Because of overpriced parking.

16. A. A sick leave notice.
    B. Frank's health problems.
    C. The best way to approach Frank.
    D. The reasons for Frank's absences.

17. A. They have no time to clean up the house.
    B. They haven't begun preparing lunch for their guests.
    C. One of their family members may not come.
    D. The little boy might damage something.

18. A. Sleep problems caused by stress.
    B. A lack of nutrition.
    C. An unpleasant side effect.
    D. Anxiety about the future.

19. A. A land developer.
    B. A senior colleague.
    C. An art dealer.
    D. An interior decorator.

20. A. A biography.
    B. A mystery.
    C. A romance.
    D. A travel guide.

21. A. He'll send it in a package.
    B. He'll write a review of it.
    C. He'll share it with someone else.
    D. He'll consider reading it.

22. A. At a school reunion.
    B. At an outdoor concert.
    C. At a religious ceremony.
    D. At an academic conference.

23. A. He hoped she could fulfill a promise.
    B. He needs information from a speech he missed.
    C. He has a proposal to make to her.
    D. He wanted her to attend an event.

24.

Candidate	Department	Experience
Charles Lee	Law	Student representative
Susan Kim	History	None
Dennis Walter	Medicine	Candidate in 55th and 56th elections
Eric Morgan	Sociology	Current president of Student Union

A. Charles Lee.
B. Susan Kim.
C. Dennis Walter.
D. Eric Morgan.

25.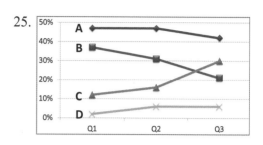

A. Line A.
B. Line B.
C. Line C.
D. Line D.

Please turn to the next page. ❯

L L L L L

Part III: Talks

In Part III, you will hear several talks. After each talk, you will hear two to three questions about the talk. After you hear each question, read the four choices in your test booklet and choose the best answer to the question you have heard.

Example:

You will hear: If you thought memory foam mattresses were not affordable, the Sleep House will change your mind. Memory foam was invented by NASA for use by astronauts in the 1960s. It helped cushion the extreme forces they experienced during take-off and their return to Earth. Memory foam mattresses were introduced to the market in the '90s. At that time, their high price kept them out of reach of most consumers, but those days are over. A queen-size memory foam mattress now starts at just NT$6,000, and a king-size one at just NT$7,500. So, why wait? Give this innovative technology a try. You'll never go back to a conventional mattress. Call the Sleep House now at 0800-255-908.

Question number 1: What information about this product does the commercial provide?

You will read: A. How it's made.
B. How long it'll last.
C. Who first used it.
D. What health benefits it has.

The best answer to the question "What information about this product does the commercial provide?" is C: "Who first used it." Therefore, you should choose answer C.

Now listen to another question based on the same talk.

You will hear: Question number 2: What can be inferred about this product from the commercial?

You will read: A. It's available in three different sizes.
B. All sizes are sold at the same price.
C. Customers get a discount if they pay cash.
D. Its price has come down substantially.

The best answer to the question "What can be inferred about this product from the commercial?" is D: "Its price has come down substantially." Therefore, you should choose answer D.

26. A. To provide details about a planned activity.
    B. To outline rules for using a campground.
    C. To promote a tour of a national park.
    D. To describe a trip down a dangerous river.

27. A. It'll be interrupted by frequent rest stops.
    B. It'll follow a circular route.
    C. It'll be shorter than tomorrow's.
    D. It'll be quite exhausting.

28. A. To suggest some repairs to Peter's car.
    B. To inform Peter of a car that's for sale.
    C. To list the advantages of a German car.
    D. To give Peter the use of her car.

29. A. Some parts have recently been replaced.
    B. The interior is very luxurious.
    C. There's nothing seriously wrong with it.
    D. It's a popular model.

30. A. Poorly maintained seats.
    B. Damage caused by spectators.
    C. A threat to hygiene.
    D. Inconsistent dimensions.

31. A. Birds of prey.
    B. Remote control aircraft.
    C. Poisonous chemicals.
    D. Radar transmitters.

32. A. Benefits and drawbacks of bulbs.
    B. A comparison of different types of bulbs.
    C. Guidance on planting and purchasing bulbs.
    D. An account of the popularity of bulbs.

33. A. The fertility of the soil.
    B. Its width and length.
    C. The pests that breed in it.
    D. Its proximity to water.

34. A. Its physical appearance.
    B. Its origin.
    C. Its smell.
    D. Its moisture.

Please turn to the next page.

35-37.

Room	Tasks	Done
12-A	Fix front door lock	✓
6-B	Handle noise complaint	✗
7-B	?	✓
9-A	Repair smoke alarm	✓

35. A. A real estate agent.
    B. A fire safety inspector.
    C. A prospective tenant.
    D. A building manager.

36. A. Collect overdue payment.
    B. Identify source of leak.
    C. Complete basic repairs.
    D. Issue parking permit.

37. A. Its cause has been identified.
    B. A technician has failed to arrive.
    C. Its consequences have been
       calculated.
    D. A legal dispute has been settled.

38-40.

Time	Paper Presentation	
	Speaker(s)	Location
1:10	Daniel Brown	Main Auditorium
2:30	Chuck Stein	South Hall
3:30	Julia Yeh	East Hall
4:30	Mary Robinson	Central Hall

38. A. To introduce a facility.
    B. To praise two staff members.
    C. To congratulate the organizer.
    D. To explain a change.

39. A. In Main Auditorium.
    B. In South Hall.
    C. In East Hall.
    D. In Central Hall.

40. A. At 1:10.
    B. At 2:30.
    C. At 3:30.
    D. At 4:30.

-The End-

R R R R R

READING COMPREHENSION TEST

This is a three-part test with forty multiple-choice questions. Each question has four choices. Special instructions will be provided for each part. You will have fifty minutes to complete this test.

Part I: Sentence Completion

In this part of the test, there are ten incomplete sentences. Beneath each sentence you will see four words or phrases, marked A, B, C and D. You are to choose the word or phrase that best completes the sentence.

Please turn to the next page. ❯

1. This valley offers some prime spots for viewing the awesome _____ of the monarch butterfly migration.
   A. trophy
   B. spectacle
   C. outrage
   D. vibration

2. Linda gave away her leather sofa because it _____ too much space in her apartment.
   A. took up
   B. filled out
   C. put away
   D. stood for

3. The Liberal Party enjoyed wide public support and was predicted to win _____ victory in the election.
   A. an underlying
   B. a simultaneous
   C. a renowned
   D. an overwhelming

4. As part of routine maintenance, technicians _____ inspect every computer on the department's network.
   A. conversely
   B. exclusively
   C. periodically
   D. tentatively

5. Although not as common as fifty years ago, arranged marriages are still _____ in parts of China.
   A. redundant
   B. reckless
   C. prevalent
   D. perpetual

6. The mayor's comments were supposed to be _____, but the media quoted them in many news reports.
   A. off the record
   B. out of order
   C. on the rise
   D. out of the blue

7. The volcano has _____ more than thirty times in recorded history. Once it even buried a town in several feet of ash.
   A. revolted
   B. faltered
   C. crumbled
   D. erupted

8. A non-smoker who breathes second-hand smoke is exposed to _____ 3,700 chemicals.
   A. frankly
   B. roughly
   C. solely
   D. briefly

9. The United Nations passed a resolution _____ the country for conducting a nuclear test last week.
   A. condemning
   B. ascertaining
   C. irritating
   D. nominating

10. Please make an appointment if you wish to discuss your investment options in _____ with one of our financial advisers.
    A. need
    B. effect
    C. depth
    D. all

Please turn to the next page. ⟩

Part II: Cloze

In this part of the test, you will read two passages. Each passage contains five missing words, phrases, or sentences. Beneath each passage, you will see five items, each with four choices, marked A, B, C and D. You are to choose the best answer for each missing word, phrase, or sentence in the two passages.

Questions 11-15

Hand-made glass beads have played an important role in the culture of the Paiwan, one of Taiwan's native aboriginal tribes. Traditionally, these ornaments were the property of upper-class members of the Paiwan tribe,   (11)   them on ceremonial occasions.   (12)   their heritage, each generation of tribal leaders passed their beads down to their children. In the twentieth century, though, this particular aspect of Paiwan culture declined. Many of the tribe's precious bead collections were broken up,   (13)   individual beads were sold to buyers in cities. In the 1980s, members of the tribe took it upon themselves to   (14)   the Paiwan bead culture and the bead-making art. Through trial and error, they developed their own techniques for making traditional as well as modern bead designs. Their creations were so successful with tourists that a bead-making industry was established.   (15)   This business also secures a key part of Paiwan culture for the future.

11. A. and wore
    B. who wore
    C. have worn
    D. were wearing

12. A. Regardless of preserving
    B. Being preserved
    C. In order to preserve
    D. By means of preserving

13. A. yet
    B. as
    C. whether
    D. only if

14. A. subscribe
    B. provoke
    C. testify
    D. revive

15. A. Today it provides employment for trained aboriginal artists in Paiwan villages.
    B. Elders usually wear single strings of white beads made of pearl or ivory around their neck.
    C. To improve revenue, the factory has started giving tours and opened a craft shop.
    D. The traditional ones bear ancient designs that look aesthetically pleasing and powerful.

Questions 16-20

Piracy has become a critical danger to fishing boats and cargo ships in the waters off the coast of Somalia. Part of the problem is __(16)__ for two decades this African country has lacked a well-organized central government. As a result, many Somalis who are struggling __(17)__ resort to robbing ships. Rather than __(18)__, Somali gunmen traveling in speed boats have been seizing ships with the intent of obtaining ransoms for the release of hostages. With the aim of countering this menace, the world's major naval powers have sent warships to __(19)__ the vulnerable shipping lanes. Experts caution that attempts to combat piracy must not be restricted to the high seas. Since piracy __(20)__ to poverty and weak governments on land, naval power alone is unlikely to eliminate this crime. Such a response must be combined with diplomatic and humanitarian measures.

16. A. during which
    B. by the time
    C. why
    D. that

17. A. being survived
    B. by surviving
    C. to survive
    D. having to survive

18. A. carrying sophisticated weapons
    B. stealing cargo from vessels
    C. recruiting desperate youth
    D. launching attacks at midnight

19. A. deport
    B. avert
    C. patrol
    D. trigger

20. A. is linked
    B. to be linked
    C. having linked
    D. should have linked

Part III: Reading Comprehension

In this part of the test, you will find several tasks. Each task contains one or two passages or charts, which are followed by two to six questions. You are to choose the best answer, A, B, C or D, to each question on the basis of the information you read.

Questions 21-22

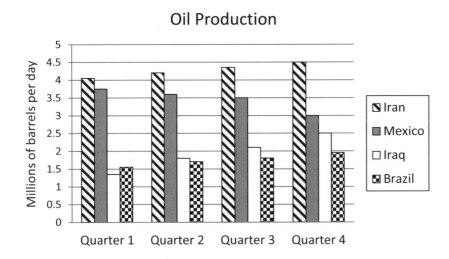

21. What information about the four countries can be learned from the chart?
    A. The ratio of their daily oil output to global oil production
    B. The amount of oil imported daily from four countries
    C. The increase in their daily oil consumption over four quarters
    D. The average daily oil output over four quarters

22. Which of the following statements is true based on the chart?
    A. In the second quarter, oil production in Mexico was half of that in Iraq.
    B. In the third quarter, oil production in all of the countries except Iran rose.
    C. Oil production in Iraq surpassed that in Brazil in three of the quarters.
    D. Oil production in Iran and Mexico rocketed dramatically in the fourth quarter.

Questions 23-25

In the 1950s, an English bird lover named Sir Peter Scott introduced ruddy ducks from the U.S. into Britain. A small number of them escaped and bred in the wild. By the early 1990s, they had spread to Spain, arousing fears that they could threaten another duck species.

After ruddy ducks had established themselves in Spain, a hybrid duck species emerged. This came about because ruddy ducks mated not only with their own species, but also with other closely-related ducks. One of these was the white-headed duck, an endangered species in Europe. Given the ruddy duck's aggressive mating behavior, there are concerns that the hybrid species could eventually replace white-headed ducks completely. This has been seen in New Zealand where the introduction of mallards resulted in the catastrophic decline of the native grey duck due to hybridization.

Since 2000, the British government has begun destroying all of the approximately 6,000 ruddy ducks in Britain. Spain followed suit soon afterwards. While the officials admit that this step is regrettable, they maintain that it is the only way to ensure the survival of the white-headed ducks. Meanwhile, opponents of the measure assert that the main danger to white-headed ducks is not breeding with ruddy ducks. Excessive hunting and destruction of their native habitat in Spain are more serious threats. They also call it unacceptable to eliminate one bird species in order to save another.

23. What is the main subject of this article?
    A. Opposition to international trading of birds
    B. The potential harm of importing a bird species
    C. The evolution of various ducks in Europe
    D. Differences between ruddy and white-headed ducks

24. Why are New Zealand's mallards and grey ducks mentioned in the second
    paragraph?
    A. To imply that a parallel scenario may happen in Europe
    B. To prove that migratory birds are declining on a global scale
    C. To compare the behavior of the birds in New Zealand and Britain
    D. To draw attention to conservation efforts in New Zealand

25. According to the article, what do the opponents of the government's policy believe?
    A. The breeding of ruddy ducks in Spain must be stopped.
    B. Both ruddy and white-headed ducks should be preserved.
    C. White-headed ducks are an exotic species from the U.S.
    D. Ruddy and white-headed ducks are genetically identical.

Please turn to the next page. ➤

Questions 26-29

While the developed world is suffering from an economic downturn, India is undergoing a period of economic progress similar to that experienced by China over the last thirty years. Analysts forecast that in three years' time, the South Asian giant will post annual GDP growth of 8%, outpacing China's 6%.

Economic reforms enacted during the 1990s are one reason for this surge. India's import tariffs were slashed, and constraints on the entry of foreign firms into Indian markets were removed. Domestic enterprises now operate in a more competitive setting, and they have shown they are ready for the challenge. India's low labor costs and high education level are also working in its favor.

Perhaps the most important factor in India's rise is the composition of its population. In ten years, the number of Indians between the ages of 15 and 64 is expected to exceed one billion. In China, however, this segment of the population will drop by 21 million to 984.4 million. In addition, the number of Indians living in towns and cities should reach 600 million in twenty years, more than double the 290 million measured in the census conducted less than two decades ago. These city dwellers will provide labor for industry and push demand for consumer products.

Pessimists warn that India must tackle certain issues if its growth is to be sustained. The nation's rail network is inadequate, and power outages occur almost daily. Despite these urgent problems, most observers expect India to transform itself in the coming decades.

26. What is this article mainly about?
    A. Current social class inequality in India
    B. The crisis of India's population explosion
    C. India's ambition to lift average living standards
    D. An analysis of India's economic prospects

27. According to the article, what change took place in India during the 1990s?
    A. Restraints on overseas enterprises were loosened.
    B. Large firms expanded their market share.
    C. Local investors were compensated for their losses.
    D. Manufacturing exports were halted temporarily.

28. What can be inferred about India's population from this article?
    A. The average age has been falling steadily.
    B. Households in rural regions are struggling with poverty.
    C. It will concentrate further in metropolitan areas.
    D. Its rapid increase is a result of mass immigration.

29. How does the writer conclude this article?
    A. By giving advice on the control of the birth rate
    B. By pressing India's leaders to upgrade health care
    C. By stressing the importance of curbing extra spending
    D. By pointing out the defects of India's infrastructure

R R R R R

← → ↻ ⌂ | 🔍 www.icmss.org.tw/conference | _ □ ✕

The Fifth International Conference on Management and Social Sciences (ICMSS)
Call for Papers

The ICMSS, now in its fifth year, is a platform for scholars to discuss research in the fields of Communication & Society, Politics & Law, Banking & Finance, and Marketing & Management.

The Fifth ICMSS will take place in Taipei, Taiwan. Researchers at universities, colleges or research institutes are invited to submit original papers to the following email account: papers@icmss.org.tw. Only upon payment of the registration fee (US$110) will submissions be reviewed for inclusion at this year's conference. All submissions will be peer reviewed by three competent referees. Authors of accepted papers may be required to amend their work as advised by the review panel. Revised papers must be submitted by the deadline below.

Important dates
Deadline for paper submission: July 1
Notification of acceptance: August 20
Deadline for submission of revised papers: September 20
Conference dates: November 10-12

Notes
For format guidelines, please click here. Papers that do not conform to the requirements will be returned for modification.

If you have questions, please write to Judy Hall at jh@icmss.org.tw.

R R R R R

From:	Dennis Burton <dburton@univmail.edu>
To:	Judy Hall <jh@icmss.org.tw>
Subject:	Questions about the 5th ICMSS

Dear Ms. Hall,

Thank you for your prompt response. I have paid the registration fee as per your instructions. However, in my previous email, I also asked whether submission of multiple articles is accepted. I hope you can clarify this as soon as possible. Both articles I plan to submit are co-authored with my colleague Professor R. Jones. Although the papers both concern the role of central banks in managing the money supply, they are written from different perspectives. I believe that they will be of great interest to the target audience of this conference.

In addition, there still appears to be a problem with the link on the website. I have tried the web browser you suggested, but I still received a "Cannot find expected page" notification.

Thank you for your assistance. I look forward to hearing from you.

Best regards,
Dennis Burton

30. What is the main purpose of the notice?
    A. To announce a chance to win a valuable scholarship
    B. To welcome conference participants to a banquet
    C. To seek contributions to an academic event
    D. To specify the theme of an annual seminar

31. What might some researchers receive on August 20?
    A. Invitations to give speeches to undergraduate students
    B. Suggestions to enhance the quality of manuscripts
    C. Cash rewards for assisting in the preparation of a meeting
    D. Reminders about equipment that will be provided

32. When did Dennis write the email?
    A. Before July 1
    B. On August 20
    C. In mid September
    D. After November 12

33. What can be inferred about Dennis?
    A. His initial inquiries were fully answered.
    B. His colleague introduced Ms. Hall to him.
    C. He has yet to complete a course of study.
    D. He has written two articles on similar topics.

34. Which feature of the ICMSS website does Dennis report as NOT functioning as expected?
    A. One that enables applicants to pay a fee
    B. One that describes key committee members
    C. One that refers to standards to be followed
    D. One that outlines the process of registration

R R R R R

Please turn to the next page for questions number 35 to 40.

Questions 35-40

Studies have shown that the earth is warming as a consequence of carbon emissions. Carbon dioxide (CO_2) is released when power is generated by burning fossil fuels, such as coal, oil, or natural gas. The rising level of CO_2 in the atmosphere is causing it to retain more energy radiated by the earth. Therefore, the
(5) earth's atmosphere is warming, bringing about climatic change.

Some governments are committed to reducing atmospheric warming by reducing carbon emissions. For that to happen, heavy industries must cut their consumption of fossil fuels. Some economists recommend using "cap and trade" to achieve this goal. In this system, each company purchases an official permit,
(10) allowing its factories or other facilities to emit CO_2 into the atmosphere. To operate, a large corporation may need to buy thousands of such permits worth millions of dollars. Cap and trade is meant to limit the total CO_2 that is produced. Unfortunately, this method is extremely complicated. It is also expensive for consumers since firms cover the cost of their permits by charging more for their
(15) merchandise and services.

An alternative to limiting carbon emissions with fewer detrimental consequences is to adopt the "carbon taxes approach." A carbon tax is either a tax on a specific fossil fuel, such as coal, or a tax on electricity that is generated using fossil fuels. Such a tax convinces both companies and consumers to use less energy
(20) from fossil fuels. The more fossil fuels or electricity a firm consumes, the higher the carbon tax it must pay to the government. Thus, energy companies can deduct their carbon taxes by producing electricity using wind or solar power instead of fossil fuels. And other firms can lower their taxes by installing more efficient equipment that uses less electricity.

(25) In this approach, carbon taxes are also added to consumers' utility bills. So the more electricity a consumer consumes, the more tax he or she is charged. Like companies, consumers can pay lower carbon taxes by using less electricity. This motivates them to abandon wasteful habits and install energy-efficient appliances and light bulbs in their homes.

(30) Carbon taxes do more than just cut consumption of fossil fuels. They also provide capital for environmental and charitable projects. Funds collected through carbon taxes can be used to finance the advancement of "green" products and technologies. Alternatively, they can be employed to fight hunger or disease around the globe. With so many advantages, carbon taxes are clearly a better choice.

35. What is the main purpose of this article?
    A. To identify factors leading to deteriorating air quality
    B. To outline a strategy related to tax avoidance
    C. To defend a project aimed at restoring household electricity
    D. To contrast schemes for discouraging the use of fossil fuels

36. What is true about the phenomenon described in the first paragraph?
    A. It occurs periodically in nature.
    B. Its cause is already understood.
    C. It depletes natural resources.
    D. Its impact is diminishing.

37. Which of the following disadvantages does the writer indicate about the cap and trade method?
    A. It is impractical.
    B. It incurs enormous debts.
    C. It is strongly biased.
    D. It takes time to get a permit.

38. What does the cap and trade method cause companies to do?
    A. Remedy their deficits
    B. Raise their retail prices
    C. Lay off employees in difficult times
    D. Form long-standing partnerships

39. What does the writer explain about carbon taxes in this article?
    A. How they promote the acceptance of renewable energy
    B. Why authorities have insisted on modifying this system
    C. How they are related to wage earners' income
    D. Why their significance is overestimated

40. What does "they" in line 33 refer to?
    A. Joint ventures
    B. Medical facilities
    C. Financial assets
    D. Instant cures

-The End-

聽力與閱讀測驗解答

聽力測驗解答

Part I		Part II		Part III	
題 號	正 答	題 號	正 答	題 號	正 答
1	C	11	A	26	A
2	A	12	C	27	D
3	C	13	B	28	B
4	A	14	D	29	C
5	B	15	B	30	C
6	D	16	C	31	A
7	B	17	D	32	C
8	C	18	C	33	B
9	D	19	D	34	A
10	B	20	A	35	D
		21	D	36	A
		22	D	37	A
		23	C	38	D
		24	A	39	B
		25	B	40	D

閱讀能力測驗解答

Part I		Part II		Part III	
題 號	正 答	題 號	正 答	題 號	正 答
1	B	11	B	21	D
2	A	12	C	22	C
3	D	13	B	23	B
4	C	14	D	24	A
5	C	15	A	25	B
6	A	16	D	26	D
7	D	17	C	27	A
8	B	18	B	28	C
9	A	19	C	29	D
10	C	20	A	30	C
				31	B
				32	A
				33	D
				34	C
				35	D
				36	B
				37	A
				38	B
				39	A
				40	C

※「全民英檢」中高級聽力、閱讀測驗採電腦閱卷，滿分 120 分。聽力測驗每題 3 分，閱讀測驗每題 3 分。為使歷次測驗的成績可以直接進行比較，考生成績將根據粗分（答對題數乘以每題分數）透過統計方式調整，以維持測驗成績的可比性。

聽力測驗錄音內容

The test is about to begin. If you have any problem with the volume of the recording, please raise your hand now.

GENERAL ENGLISH PROFICIENCY TEST
HIGH-INTERMEDIATE LEVEL LISTENING COMPREHENSION TEST

This listening comprehension test will test your ability to understand spoken English. In this test, each conversation, talk and question will be spoken JUST ONE TIME. They will not be written out for you. There are three parts to this test. Special instructions will be given to you at the beginning of each part.

Part I: Answering Questions

In Part I, you will hear ten questions. After you hear a question, read the four choices in your test booklet and decide which one is the best answer to the question you have heard.

Example:

You will hear: I heard all flights to Penghu have been delayed due to thick fog at the airport.

You will read: A.   When will the sky there clear up?
                    B.   Is the engine still out of order?
                    C.   How did they lose the luggage?
                    D.   Could it be the only aisle seat?

The best answer to the question "I heard all flights to Penghu have been delayed due to thick fog at the airport." is A: "When will the sky there clear up?" Therefore, you should choose answer A.

The test is about to begin. If you have any problem with the volume of the recording, please raise your hand now.

Please turn to the next page.

Now let us begin Part I with question number 1.

1. When was the last time you saw the doctor?

2. Sir, would you mind explaining that equation again? It's puzzling me.

3. You've been in town for a month. Why haven't you come to see us before now?

4. The elevator is broken, so we'll have to use the stairs.

5. Can't you turn down the volume? Who can concentrate with all that noise?

6. You always work so late. How often do you eat at home?

7. Was Lydia trying to persuade her mother to let her study architecture in Spain for a year?

8. I heard that you've received a job offer from Jackson and Brothers Enterprises.

9. Has the new contract been signed by both companies?

10. The thing I find annoying about politicians is that they never give a straight answer.

Part II: Conversations

In Part II, you will hear several conversations between a man and a woman. After each conversation, you will hear one to two questions about the conversation. After you hear the question, read the four choices in your test booklet and choose the best answer to the question you have heard.

Example:

<u>You will hear:</u>

(Woman)	I want to make a fruit salad for the picnic tomorrow.
(Man)	Okay, how about these bananas?
(Woman)	No, they're too green and too firm.
(Man)	Why don't we buy these dragon fruit? They look ready to eat.
(Woman)	Good, get two of those. The mangos are nice and soft, too; let's grab one.

Question: On what basis are the speakers selecting ingredients?

<u>You will read:</u>
A. How ripe the items are.
B. How their flavors will blend.
C. How expensive each variety is.
D. How long it takes to prepare them.

The best answer to the question "On what basis are the speakers selecting ingredients?" is A: "How ripe the items are." Therefore, you should choose answer A.

Please turn to the next page. Now let us begin Part II with question number 11.

11. M: Where did this painting come from?
    W: I painted it.
    M: Oh? I didn't know you were an artist.
    W: I'm not, really. I've only been taking lessons for a few weeks.
    M: Well, this painting does show some talent!
    W: You're teasing me.
    M: Not at all.

    Question: What kind of painter is the woman?

12. W: Are you coming to our study group meeting tonight?
    M: I don't think so. I've got to finish drafting my economics report before Tuesday. I want to concentrate on that first, and then I'll begin focusing on the biology exam.
    W: In case you change your mind, we'll be in the study lounge on the fourth floor of the dormitory from eight to eleven.

    Question: What is the man planning to do this evening?

13. W: Look, over there. Do you see the tall white one with the black head?
    M: No. Hand me the binoculars.
    W: It's in the water at the edge of the pond.
    M: Oh, I see it now. Its beak is quite long and curved.
    W: Do you recognize the species?
    M: I'm not familiar with it. You'd better take a photo so we can identify it later.

    Question: What are the speakers doing?

14. W: Bill, I'm calling about the question you asked at the meeting today.
    M: Oh, about whether the cost analysis would be done by the end of this week.
    W: Yes, that's right. It looks like we'll have it for you on Friday.
    M: That's great. I'd like to review it over the weekend, before my business trip.
    W: You're leaving on Monday, right?
    M: Actually, I'm leaving Sunday evening.

    Question: Why does Bill need the report this week?

15. W: Isn't this a tourist town?

M: It was at one time, but hardly anyone visits it anymore.

W: Why is that?

M: The main highway used to go through the town. So people would stop along their way to have lunch or visit the shops. But then, the bypass was built. Now, few tourists stop.

W: Because they're eager to get to their destinations.

M: Exactly.

Question: Why have tourists stopped visiting the town?

16. M: If I'm not mistaken, Frank has taken more sick leave than any other employee.

W: It's true. I got a report from personnel last week about this very matter.

M: Have you spoken to Frank about it yet?

W: Not yet. I'm considering how to bring it up without embarrassing him.

M: I favor the direct approach. After all, his job may be on the line.

W: You may be right.

Question: What are the two speakers mainly discussing?

17. M: When will Bob and Alice arrive for lunch?

W: At 12:00, and they're bringing their son along.

M: How old is he?

W: Two, and he's very active.

M: In that case, we'd better put everything fragile out of his reach.

W: Like the antique vase on the table?

M: That's right. I'll put it in the closet right now.

Question: What are these people concerned about?

18. W: David, you seem very tired. Didn't you get enough sleep?

M: No, I got plenty of sleep. It's this medicine I'm taking for my cold. There's something in it that makes me feel really drowsy.

W: Perhaps a cup of coffee would help you stay awake.

M: I've already had two cups of coffee today.

Question: What is David suffering from?

19. W: Patricia Hawkins just called.

M: Is she ready to meet with us?

W: Yes, she's finished a space plan for our living room. She also has some pictures of furniture selections she'd like to propose.

M: Good. When can we meet?

W: She suggested Saturday morning at ten.

M: That's fine with me.

W: OK, I'll let her know.

Question: Who is the woman going to call?

(Questions number 20 and 21 are based on the following conversation.)

M: That's the book you got at the airport?

W: Yes. It's about the legendary actor Cary Grant. It's not the sort of thing I normally read.

M: You usually bring mysteries on our diving trips.

W: I didn't see any that caught my interest.

M: A lot has already been written about Cary Grant. Does the author have anything new to offer?

W: In fact, I've only read the first couple of chapters, and they mostly deal with his unhappy upbringing. His mother was hospitalized with depression.

M: How did he get into entertainment?

W: Believe it or not, he started out working in a circus, and later worked the lights for a magician.

M: Maybe I'll look at it after you're finished.

Question number 20: Which type of book are the speakers discussing?

Question number 21: What does the man imply about the woman's book?

(Questions number 22 and 23 are based on the following conversation.)

W: Carson, how are you? It's good to see you again.

M: Helena, I was hoping to see you here. Are you just arriving?

W: Yes, I got a late start this morning. I missed the opening remarks and half of the plenary speech. I was sitting in the back. I didn't want to disturb anyone by coming to the front while the speaker was at the podium.

M: You know, I've been thinking of sending you an email about a paper we might collaborate on.

W: Really? I'd love to hear more. I need to publish something this year, but I haven't found a suitable topic to work on.

M: Then this is a great opportunity. Shall we discuss it over lunch?

W: Absolutely.

Question number 22: Where are the speakers?

Question number 23: Why was the man looking forward to talking with the woman?

(For question number 24, please look at the table.)

W: Tomorrow we'll vote for the president of the student union, but I still haven't decided who I'll cast my ballot for.

M: One of the candidates is from your department. Aren't you going to support her?

W: Susan? No. She's just a freshman. I don't think she could handle the issues that are going on in the university.

M: I supported the candidate from the Department of Medicine the past two years, but he has never been elected. I think I'll vote for someone else this time, maybe the guy from the law department. His record of standing up for student interests in meetings with school governors really impresses me.

W: What about the current president? He's popular.

M: Well, his close connection with the university's board of directors concerns me.

Question: Which candidate will the man most likely vote for in the election?

(For question number 25, please look at the chart.)

W: As you can see from the chart, while Asia remained the major source of customers for our hotels, the percentage dropped in the last quarter.

M: Wasn't that expected? We shifted more of our advertising budget to North America and Europe.

W: Yes, but the proportion of reservations made in the U.S. and Canada actually declined sharply, while the share in Europe increased greatly.

M: So we need to figure out why North American guests were staying away.

Question: Which line in the chart refers to North American guests?

Part III: Talks

In Part III, you will hear several talks. After each talk, you will hear two to three questions about the talk. After you hear each question, read the four choices in your test booklet and choose the best answer to the question you have heard.

Example:

You will hear: If you thought memory foam mattresses were not affordable, the Sleep House will change your mind. Memory foam was invented by NASA for use by astronauts in the 1960s. It helped cushion the extreme forces they experienced during take-off and their return to Earth. Memory foam mattresses were introduced to the market in the '90s. At that time, their high price kept them out of reach of most consumers, but those days are over. A queen-size memory foam mattress now starts at just NT$6,000, and a king-size one at just NT$7,500. So, why wait? Give this innovative technology a try. You'll never go back to a conventional mattress. Call the Sleep House now at 0800-255-908.

Question number 1:   What information about this product does the commercial provide?

You will read: A.   How it's made.
B.   How long it'll last.
C.   Who first used it.
D.   What health benefits it has.

The best answer to the question "What information about this product does the commercial provide?" is C: "Who first used it." Therefore, you should choose answer C.

Now listen to another question based on the same talk.

You will hear: Question number 2:   What can be inferred about this product from the commercial?

You will read: A.   It's available in three different sizes.
B.   All sizes are sold at the same price.
C.   Customers get a discount if they pay cash.
D.   Its price has come down substantially.

The best answer to the question "What can be inferred about this product from the commercial?" is D: "Its price has come down substantially." Therefore, you should choose answer D. Now let us begin Part III with question number 26.

(Questions number 26 and 27 are based on the following announcement.)

Can I have your attention, everyone? Tomorrow, we're going to hike to the bottom of the Grand Canyon, where we'll camp overnight beside the Colorado River. The trail we're going to take is about eleven kilometers long, so the hike down will take us about three hours. Besides your camping gear, bring along at least three liters of water since there will be none available until we reach the campground. Now, tomorrow's hike will be much easier than the trip back up on Wednesday. That will take us about eight hours, so be prepared for a real workout. Are there any questions? If not, we'll meet back here at 6:00 A.M.

Question number 26: What is the main purpose of this announcement?

Question number 27: What does the speaker point out about the hike on Wednesday?

(Questions number 28 and 29 are based on the following telephone message.)

Peter? This is Joan. You told me recently that you were interested in buying a used car. Well, I may have found the perfect one for you. It belongs to the German couple that live upstairs. They mentioned to me today that they'll be moving back to Germany soon and intend to sell their car. They bought it seven years ago but it's still in excellent condition, as they haven't driven it very far, only about 25,000 kilometers. It has a two-liter engine, seats five people comfortably, and they're asking NT$150,000, which is in your price range. If you're interested, I'll arrange a time when you can look at the car and test drive it. Bye.

Question number 28: Why did the speaker leave this telephone message?

Question number 29: What does the speaker imply about the car?

(Questions number 30 and 31 are based on the following lecture.)

Every summer, the Wimbledon tennis championships take place in Britain. This three-week event is attended by half a million people. Years ago, the tournament also attracted hundreds of pigeons, which feasted on crumbs left behind by spectators. While looking for food, the pigeons would fly around the courts and dirty them with their droppings. One year, organizers hired Apex Control, which offered a brilliant solution. Apex Control uses hawks to keep pigeons away from airports and other sites. During the next Wimbledon tournament, a handler flew a hawk around the courts several times before matches began. That was enough to scare the pigeons away. Since then, the hawks have visited Wimbledon every summer. And the pigeons have ceased to be a problem.

Question number 30: What were the event organizers most likely concerned about at the venue?

Question number 31: According to this lecture, what is used by Apex Control at various places?

(Questions number 32 to 34 are based on the following talk.)

If you have a garden, then you may want to consider tulips and other blooming plants that grow from bulbs. Generally speaking, the ideal time to plant bulbs is in the fall. Before you start, measure the area that you will plant. Accurate measurements can help you decide how many bulbs you should buy since each bulb type requires a different amount of space to thrive. Choose bulbs that reflect your preferences in terms of color, height, bloom time, and ability to grow in sun or shade. To ensure that the bulbs you choose will produce more blooms, select them carefully. Pick those that are free of bruises and soft spots. Later, when you're ready to plant, follow the instructions on the bulb package.

Question number 32: What does this talk mainly provide?

Question number 33: According to this talk, what should people know about the plot of land in which bulbs will be planted?

Question number 34: Which factor influences the number of blooms that a bulb will produce?

(For questions number 35 to 37, please look at the progress report.)

Hello, Mrs. Stuart. This is Matthew Morris. I've sent you a progress report on the issues you wanted me to look into. I took care of the problem with 12-A yesterday. The tenant's key got stuck in the lock, so we had a locksmith install a new lock. As for the complaint about a strange noise from the ceiling of 6-B, I haven't been able to get in touch with the tenant. I put a note in her mailbox, and I expect she will contact me when she returns. Then the tenant in 7-B gave me the rent he owed last night. Finally, I examined the smoke alarm in 9-A. There was nothing seriously wrong. The batteries just needed to be replaced.

Question number 35: Who is this message most likely intended for?

Question number 36: Based on the message, which item should appear in the shaded area?

Question number 37: What does the speaker imply about the problem in 9-A?

(For questions number 38 to 40, please look at the agenda.)

Welcome back. I've got two announcements. There have been several alterations to today's schedule. If you have today's program with you, I suggest you take notes. First, because of a problem with the air conditioning in East Hall, Ms. Julia Yeh's presentation scheduled to begin at 3:30 will be held in Central Hall instead. We apologize for the inconvenience, but your comfort is a priority. Next, there was an error in the program. Two speakers' names were switched. The upcoming presentation at 2:30 will be given by Dr. Mary Robinson, not Dr. Chuck Stein. All right. I appreciate everyone's patience, and now let's welcome the speaker of this session, Dr. Mary Robinson, to the stage.

Question number 38: What is the purpose of the speaker's first announcement?

Question number 39: Where is this announcement most likely being given?

Question number 40: According to the announcement, when will Dr. Chuck Stein's session begin?

This is the end of the listening comprehension test.

Note

學習指南

ANSWERING QUESTIONS

中高級聽力

第一部份

問答

這部份包含日常生活中常見的十個問句與直述句,聽完之後根據題目的語意選擇最適當的回應。

本部份評量的學習表現包括:

✓ 能理解日常生活、學校或工作情境中常用詞彙與各式句型

✓ 能依據句子的語意與情境選擇適當的回應

✓ 能辨識句子語調所表達的情緒與態度

🖋 考前提醒

這個部份評量考生是否具備理解常見的口語句型與詞彙的能力,並選擇出適當的回應,以有效應對生活情境,展現溝通互動的素養。評量內容與日常生活、學校生活及工作情境相關。建議平時多熟悉口語中各式句型與常用詞彙及其正確發音,練習迅速完整地理解語意與情境,避免僅憑句中一兩個字拼湊猜測答案。

作答時

1. **首先掌握題目的句型 (例如 Wh 問句、Yes-No 問句與直述句) 與語言溝通功能。** 熟悉這些句型與溝通功能,有助於即時理解句意並選擇適當回應。

常見句型	學習建議	說明
Wh 問句	先聽清楚該句的 wh- 疑問詞，再選擇合適的回答。常見的 wh- 疑問詞包含 who、what、when、where、how、which、why 等。	例句 Where can I find information on your clinic's health check-up program? 可能的回應 It's available in our brochure. 說明 這個題目的 wh- 疑問詞為 where，詢問健檢資訊可在哪裡找到，而宣傳手冊上很可能會有此資訊。
Yes-No 問句	Yes-No 問句的回應主要可分為直接回答與間接回答。 1. 直接回答：包含 Yes、No 或是類似用語的肯定或否定回答，例如：Sure, no problem. 2. 間接回答：可能是不確定的回應，例如：Well, I'm not sure.，或是以另一個問句來反問，例如：Will size eleven do? Yes-No 問句不一定會用 Yes/No 回答，一定要依語意與選項內容判斷。	例句 If you happen to be free this weekend, will you go camping with us in the mountains? 可能的回應 1. Yes. I'd love to. （肯定） 2. I'm afraid I can't go. （否定） 3. Let me check my schedule. （不確定的間接回答） 4. Cool. But how's the weather looking? （以問句回應的間接回答） 說明 這個題目詢問週末是否有空去露營，因此可能的回應會針對「是否可以去」做回應。
直述句	直述句的回應和句子的情境、語意與溝通目的相關。先聽懂關鍵字了解該句情境與語意，再判斷溝通目的。常見溝通功能介紹請見下表。	例句 I heard Bangkok was voted the best Asian tourist city this year. 可能的回應 I'm considering visiting there myself. 說明 這個題目陳述與旅遊城市相關的事實，故回應會針對句中的重點資訊（the best Asian tourist city）做回應。

下表為常見的溝通功能，判斷該句的溝通功能有助於理解說話者的語意與目的，並做出適當的回應。

常見溝通功能	例句	可能回應與說明
陳述事實	Someone in our department has been spreading gossip about Harry and Sally.	陳述事實的句子可針對當中的重點資訊（gossip）回應，例如：Really? What did you hear?
表達意見／情緒	It's amazing that the warehouse has been converted into such a magnificent gallery.	說話者表達對這間畫廊的讚嘆，回應可以呼應讚嘆，例如：Indeed. It's almost unbelievable.
提出要求	That persistent salesperson is at our front door again. It's your turn to deal with him.	說話者要求聽者去應付推銷員，回應應該與這項要求有關，例如：You know I can't reject people. 此句為間接回應，表示他無法應對推銷員。
交際應酬	Mr. Lee, allow me to introduce you to Mr. William Grant.	社交場合常見的用語，故回應也會是一般社交問候用語，例如：Nice to meet you, Mr. Grant.

2. **接著仔細閱讀每個選項。**除了聽清楚題目之外，仔細閱讀選項也很重要。正答會是最適當的回應，但切勿看到誘答選項有與題目相同的字就認為是答案，要仔細讀完每個選項再選出最合適的回應。

掌握這幾個小撇步，可以減少失誤的機率唷！

第 1 題

When was the last time you saw the doctor?

A.　My appointment is next week.

B.　His clinic is very near here.

C.　I went on Monday.

D.　He was in the hospital.

你上一次看醫生是什麼時候？

A.　我預約下周。

B.　他的診所離這裡很近。

C.　我星期一去的。

D.　他在醫院。

正解 Ⓒ

本題的情境為一般日常生活對話，是 When 開始的問句，而且動詞是過去式，因此我們知道問的是發生在過去的事件。

題目問的是 When was the last time you saw the doctor?（你上一次看醫生是什麼時候？）因此與時間相關的選項 C：I went on Monday.（我星期一去的）是最合適的答案。選項 A 雖然也與時間相關，但是時間點在未來，與題意不符，而選項 B 與 D 皆與地點有關，未針對題目中的 When 回應，因此都不是正確答案。

Sir, would you mind explaining that equation again? It's puzzling me.

A. Could you wait until after class?

B. You're flattering me.

C. How on earth did you solve it?

D. I'm glad that we could work this out.

老師，你介意再解釋一次那個方程式嗎？我有點困惑。

A. 你可以等到下課後嗎？

B. 你過獎了。

C. 你到底是怎麼解題的？

D. 我很高興我們可以解決。

正解 A

本題情境為學校的數學課，是 would 開始的 Yes-No 問句，此句雖然以疑問句的形式呈現，但 Would you mind... 實際上是禮貌地提出請求。

題目中說話者希望對方可以再解釋一次方程式（explaining that equation），因此最合適的回應是選項 A：Could you wait until after class?（你可以等到下課後嗎？），其他選項皆不是針對「請求」的適合回應。

關鍵字詞 equation 方程式

第 3 題

You've been in town for a month. Why haven't you come to see us before now?

A. I'd love to. Thanks for the offer.

B. Sure. I missed your great cooking.

C. My bad. I had to get settled first.

D. No wonder. It's such a small town.

你到城裡已經一個月了，怎麼現在才來看我們？

A. 我很樂意，謝謝提議。

B. 當然，我想念你的好廚藝。

C. 我的錯，我必須要先安頓好。

D. 難怪，這真是個小城鎮。

正解 C

本題情境為一般社交場合，是直述句加上 Why 開始的問句，說話者主要是在詢問原因。

題目問 Why haven't you come to see us before now?（怎麼現在才來看我們？），而且說話者得知對方已經來一個月了，因此對方應該要解釋為何遲了一個月才來拜訪，故最適合的回應為選項 C：My bad. I had to get settled first.（我的錯，我必須先安頓好。），其他選項雖然都與題目有關，但是並未解釋延遲拜訪的原因，故不是最合適的回答。

關鍵字詞 settle 安頓

The elevator is broken, so we'll have to use the stairs.

A. At least it'll be good exercise.

B. That'll be enough, thanks.

C. Not again. I haven't saved any of them.

D. They fell down and got hurt.

電梯壞了，所以我們必須走樓梯。

A. 至少那是個好運動。

B. 那樣就夠了，謝謝。

C. 不會吧，我什麼都沒有存。

D. 他們跌倒受傷了。

正解 Ⓐ

本題情境為一般日常生活，是一句用來陳述事實的直述句，因此可針對句子中的重點資訊回應。

說話者表示電梯壞了（elevator is broken），只能走樓梯（use the stairs），因此針對這兩項訊息的其中一項做出回應。選項 A：At least it'll be good exercise.（至少那是個好運動）針對「走樓梯」回應，因此是最合適的答案。選項 B 與 C 皆與本句的情境無關，且題目並未提到跟受傷有關的事，故選項 D 也不是正確答案。

關鍵字詞 broken 故障

第 5 題

Can't you turn down the volume? Who can concentrate with all that noise?

A.　Okay. I'll check out volume two.

B.　Sorry. I didn't know it was so loud.

C.　Why not? Wasn't he listening?

D.　Of course. He can come with Louis.

你不能把音量關小聲嗎？聲音這麼大誰能專心？

A.　好的，我去借第二卷。

B.　抱歉，我不知道會這麼大聲。

C.　為何不？他沒有在聽嗎？

D.　當然，他可以跟 Louis 一起來。

正解　Ⓑ

本題情境為一般日常生活，第一句是 Can 開始的 Yes-No 問句，第二句為 Who 開始的問句，雖然都是問句形式，但是須聽懂說話者的言外之意其實是在抱怨。

本題說話者抱怨音量太大，因此回應要與音量太大相關，故選項 B：Sorry. I didn't know it was so loud.（抱歉，我不知道會這麼大聲）是最合適的答案。選項 A 的 volume，是指書籍的「卷」並非「音量」；選項 C 與 D 與題目較無關，所以都不是正確答案。

關鍵字詞　volume 音量

You always work so late. How often do you eat at home?

A. As soon as possible.

B. Around the corner.

C. For one hour.

D. Very rarely.

你總是工作到很晚。你常在家吃飯嗎？

A. 儘快

B. 快了

C. 一小時

D. 很少

正解 D

本題情境為一般社交生活，第一句為陳述事實的直述句，第二句為 How often 開始的問句，聽清楚疑問詞才不至於答非所問。

本題問 How often do you eat at home?（你常在家吃飯嗎？），因此回應要與頻率有關，故選項 D：Very rarely.（很少）是最合適的答案。其他選項雖然都與時間有關，但是並未針對 How often 回答。

第 7 題

Was Lydia trying to persuade her mother to let her study architecture in Spain for a year?

A. Yes, but she lives in a dormitory.

B. Yes, and she almost succeeded.

C. No, but I lost contact with her.

D. No, and you're not going without her.

Lydia 是不是曾試著說服她媽媽讓她在西班牙念一年建築？

A. 對，但她住在宿舍。

B. 對，她差點成功了。

C. 不，但我跟她失去聯絡。

D. 不，而且沒有她你就不能去了。

正解　B

本題情境為一般社交生活，是 Was 開始的 Yes-No 問句，描述發生在過去的事，回應皆為包含 Yes/No 的直接回答，需依語意判斷何者是最適合的回應。

說話者問 Was Lydia trying to persuade her mother to let her study architecture in Spain for a year?（Lydia 是不是曾試著說服她媽媽讓她在西班牙念一年建築？）因此最佳回應要與 Lydia 之前是否說服成功有關，故選項 B：Yes, and she almost succeeded.（對，她差點成功了）是最合適的答案。選項 A 與 D 雖與題目略為相關，但未針對過去的事件回應，C 與題意較不相關，因此都不是最合適的回應。

關鍵字詞 persuade 說服　architecture 建築

I heard that you've received a job offer from Jackson and Brothers Enterprises.

A. They haven't arrived yet.

B. When is it effective?

C. I'm still considering it, though.

D. The new recruits need training.

我聽說你得到 Jackson and Brothers 企業的工作機會。

A. 他們還沒到。

B. 何時生效？

C. 但我還在考慮。

D. 新員工需要訓練。

正解 C

本題情境為與工作相關的社交對話，是陳述事實的直述句，可以針對重點資訊（job offer）回應。

聽者得到一個工作機會，因此選項 C：I'm still considering it, though.（但我還在考慮）是最合適的回應。Jackson and Brothers 是公司名稱，並非說話者的朋友，故選項 A 不正確；而選項 B 問 When is it effective?（何時生效），但聽者是得到此工作的人，有此疑問不合理；選項 D 與工作機會較無關。

關鍵字詞 enterprise 企業

第 9 題

Has the new contract been signed by both companies?

A. Yes, I'm working on the first draft.

B. Yes, both of them canceled the meeting.

C. No, I can't decide which class to take.

D. No, they're still negotiating some details.

兩家公司都簽新合約了嗎？

A. 是的，我在擬草案。

B. 是的，兩者都取消會議。

C. 不，我無法決定要上哪堂課。

D. 不，他們還在協商一些細節。

正解　D

本題為職場相關的情境，是 Has 開始的 Yes-No 問句，四個選項皆為包含 Yes/No 的直接回答，須聽清楚句中的關鍵字詞（contract、sign）才能選出適合的回應。

本題問 Has the new contract been signed by both companies?（兩家公司都簽新合約了嗎？），選項 A 與 B 一開始先回答「是的」，但是後方的補充說明卻都是與尚未簽合約前的流程相關，故不是適合的回應。選項 C 則是與課程相關，與此情境不符，只有選項 D：No, they're still negotiating some details.（不，他們還在協商一些細節）為最合適的回應。

關鍵字詞　negotiate 協商

The thing I find annoying about politicians is that they never give a straight answer.

A. It's merely a myth.

B. I couldn't agree more.

C. A statement will be released.

D. You'd better check the source.

讓我覺得政客很討厭的是他們從不給直接的答案。

A. 它只是個迷思。

B. 非常同意。

C. 聲明將被發布。

D. 你最好檢查來源。

正解 B

本題情境為一般社交場合,是表達意見的直述句,說話者在評論政客,因此回答可以呼應說話者的意見。

本題的說話者提出他不喜歡政客的主觀看法,因此聽者須針對說話者的看法加以回應,故選項 B:I couldn't agree more.(非常同意)為最合適的答案。

關鍵字詞 straight 直接的

🔍 關鍵字詞

接著我們來複習本部份的重點詞彙

equation 名 方程式（第 2 題）

例句
- Would you mind explaining that equation again?
  你介意再解釋一次那個方程式嗎？

- The teacher demonstrated how to solve a math problem by combining two equations.
  這位老師示範如何合併方程式來解數學題。

settle 動 安頓（第 3 題）

例句
- I had to get settled first.
  我必須要先安頓好。

- Four hundred years ago, people sailed across the ocean from Fujian and settled down in Taiwan.
  四百年前，人們從福建渡海來台定居。

broken 形 故障（第 4 題）

例句
- The elevator is broken, so we'll have to use the stairs.
  電梯壞了，所以我們必須走樓梯。

- The new chairperson is determined to repair the broken company culture, starting with holding regular workshops on team building.
  新任董事長決定定期舉辦團隊建立工作坊來修復頹喪的公司文化。

volume 名 音量（第 5 題）

例句
- Can't you turn down the volume?
  你不能把音量關小聲嗎？

- Turn the volume up; otherwise, those sitting in the back will hear almost nothing.
  調高音量，否則坐在後面的人會聽不到聲音。

persuade 動 說服（第 7 題）

例句
- Was Lydia trying to persuade her mother to let her study architecture in Spain for a year?
  Lydia 是不是曾試著說服她媽媽讓她在西班牙念一年建築？

- The student leader of the English Department persuaded a clothing company to sponsor their graduation play by paying for the costumes.
  英文系的學生代表說服一家服裝公司贊助他們畢業公演的戲服。

architecture 名 建築（第 7 題）

例句
- Gothic architecture features stained glass windows and pointed arches.
  哥德式建築以彩色玻璃窗和尖肋拱頂為特色。

enterprise 名 企業（第 8 題）

例句
- I heard that you've received a job offer from Jackson and Brothers Enterprises.
  我聽說你得到 Jackson and Brothers 企業的工作機會。

- An enterprise sells products or provides services to earn profits.
  企業銷售產品或提供服務以賺取利潤。

negotiate 動 協商（第 9 題）

例句
- They're still negotiating some details.
  他們還在協商一些細節。

- After months of efforts, the corporation negotiated a loan from the bank successfully.
  在數月的努力之後，這家公司向銀行貸款成功。

straight 形 直接（第 10 題）

例句
- The thing I find annoying about politicians is that they never give a straight answer.
  讓我覺得政客很討厭的是他們從不給直接的答案。

- Instead of getting straight to the point, the mayor beat around the bush, which made his argument for a better hospital unclear.
  這位市長拐彎抹角，沒有直接講重點，反而使得改善醫院的論點不清。

💡 學習策略

1. 積極充實詞彙

要聽懂句意最重要的是理解句中的關鍵詞彙。本部份聽力內容出現的詞彙除與日常生活相關外，亦包含學校生活及工作情境。平時應具備主動探索的態度，在生活情境中隨時聯想，累積各類詞彙。例如新聞上常出現都市更新的消息，則可聯想英文的說法為 urban renewal。

2. 掌握正確發音

有些學習者在學習詞彙時僅將重點放在拼字與字義，忽略發音正確性，例如將 exhibition [ˌɛksəˋbɪʃən] 唸為 *[ˌɪksəˋbɪʃən]（母音唸錯），或是重音位置放錯，將 maintenance [ˋmentənəns] 的重音誤放在第二音節。因此在聽到該字時，反而因錯誤發音而影響理解。平時學習詞彙時，除了字義、用法及拼字外，也可善用網路科技資源，聆聽線上字典的發音並開口唸，確切掌握正確發音。

3. 熟悉口語中常用的片語及慣用語

英語使用者說話時常使用片語及慣用語，例如：pay off（帶來好結果；清償債務）、You bet!（當然）。這些詞彙通常有固定的用法與使用時機，學習新單字時，必須特別留意與這個單字相關的片語與慣用語，將有助於培養符號運用與溝通表達的能力。平日練習口語對話時也可以試著運用，這麼做的話漸漸就能熟悉用法，更可以避免明明每個字都聽清楚了，卻仍然不懂整句意思的情況。

4. 練習各種場合中常用的句型及應答方式

平日多接觸英語會話，積極參與課內外英語文團體學習活動，與老師或同學用英語對話，練習口語中各類常見的應答方式，方能迅速理解句子的語意並將學過的詞彙與句型加以活用。亦可藉由觀看英語影集與電影，觀察英語使用者在不同場合的口語表達方式，有助於迅速掌握句子的語意，並做出正確的回應。

CONVERSATIONS

中高級聽力
第二部份

對話

聽力測驗 第二部份 對話

這部份每題包含一段對話及 1-2 個相關的問題，聽完對話後，根據對話與題目的內容選擇最適當的答案。

本部份評量的學習表現包括：

- ✓ 能聽懂英語日常對話
  - ★ 能根據上下文釐清訊息
  - ★ 能分析、歸納多項訊息
  - ★ 能綜合相關資訊預測可能的發展或做合理猜測
  - ★ 能理解說話者的觀點、態度與言外之意

考前提醒

這個部份主要評量考生是否能跨越單句的層次，理解上下文的關係，以掌握對話中重要的訊息。評量的對話種類包含家庭會話、社交會話、工作或課堂討論、電話交談等，內容情境多與日常生活、學校生活及工作場合相關。

平時除了增加詞彙量以理解對話的字面意義外，建議練習不同的聽解技巧，例如：釐清上下文關係並根據語境推敲含意、整合歸納多項訊息或多篇文本中的訊息、根據對話的脈絡進行評論或詮釋，考試的時候就可以迅速理解對話內容，找到答案。

作答時，可運用以下幾個方式幫助理解、分析、統整與詮釋對話內容：

1. 記下關鍵字並運用 5W1H 分析法理解對話內容

   如要快速掌握資訊較多的對話重點，可以在聆聽對話的同時，記下所聽到的關鍵字。平常練習時，可利用 5W1H（what、who、when、where、why、how）分析法掌握對話的主題、說話者身分、何時發生、發生地點、為何發生、如何解決等（例如第 11 題）。

2. 串聯關鍵字，整合對話中的重要資訊

   對話中的關鍵訊息出現一次後，可能會再以不同的措辭重現於下文中，可利用這些同義詞，確認已知的訊息。另外，答題的相關資訊有時會分散出現於對話中（例如第 13 題），整合這些資訊即可推知正答。

3. 分析訊息之間的關聯性，釐清上下文關係

   理解對話中訊息之間的關係，才能正確掌握對話的內容。這些訊息可能以幾種較常見的方式出現，例如：詢問與回答、提議與回覆、因果關係、對比關係、分類與舉例等等。分析訊息之間的關聯性，就能迅速深入理解對話的內容（例如第 12 題）。

4. 分類資訊，歸納多項訊息

   可利用筆記分類訊息，例如：比較 A 與 B 兩個人物、地點或物品差異的這類題目，邊聽對話的同時，邊把屬於 A、B 的關鍵資訊分別歸類紀錄，可幫助釐清訊息。同理，如果題目問某件事情改變前後的差異，改變前的特點可以列在一邊、另一側則是列出改變後的特點。涉及比較的圖表題（例如第 24 題）適合以此種方式歸納訊息。

5. 推論說話者言外之意或觀點

   聆聽對話時，除了理解其字面意義外，有時也需運用自己的知識與生活經驗，建構出更完整的語意，並推論說話者的言外之意與觀點或是預測可能的發展。例如：He's not the only plumber around, you know.（這附近又不是只有他一個水電工。），雖然說話者未明確表示自己的意見，卻暗示應該另請高明。

運用這些聽解方式，多練習之後，可以更完整地理解對話內容！

(M) Where did this painting come from?

(W) I painted it.

(M) Oh? I didn't know you were an artist.

(W) I'm not, really. I've only been taking lessons for a few weeks.

(M) Well, this painting does show some talent!

(W) You're teasing me.

(M) Not at all.

What kind of painter is the woman?

A. A beginner.

B. A portrait specialist.

C. An experienced amateur.

D. A professional.

（男） 這幅畫是哪來的？

（女） 我畫的。

（男） 喔？我不知道你是個畫家。

（女） 其實我不是啦。我才上了幾個禮拜的課。

（男） 這幅畫可以看出來你很有天份！

（女） 你在逗我吧。

（男） 才沒有。

女子是哪種畫家？

A. 初學者

B. 肖像畫家

C. 經驗豐富的業餘畫家

D. 專業畫家

正解 Ⓐ

本題的情境為一般社交對話，根據字面意義理解對話，掌握對話中的幾個關鍵訊息即可得知正答。

題目問的是對話中的女生是哪種畫家。根據對話，女生否認自己是畫家（artist），表示 I've only been taking lessons for a few weeks.（我才上了幾個禮拜的課），可知她並非專業畫家、也非經驗豐富的業餘畫家；對話中也沒有提到女生的畫作主題，無從得知女生是否為肖像畫家，只有選項 A：beginner（初學者）才是符合女生的描述。

平時可利用前方提到的 5W1H 分析法練習如何快速掌握重要的對話訊息，以本題為例，可將對話中提到的重要資訊整理如下：

Where did the painting come from?	The woman painted it.
What are the speakers talking about?	A painting.
Who is the woman?	A beginner painter.
When did the woman start taking lessons?	A few weeks ago.

關鍵字詞　tease 戲弄、取笑　amateur 業餘從事者、外行

77

(W)　Are you coming to our study group meeting tonight?

（女）　你今晚會參加我們讀書會的聚會嗎？

(M)　I don't think so. I've got to finish drafting my economics report before Tuesday. I want to concentrate on that first, and then I'll begin focusing on the biology exam.

（男）　應該不會。我必須在星期二前完成經濟學報告的初稿。我想先專心完成那個，然後我得開始準備生物學考試。

(W)　In case you change your mind, we'll be in the study lounge on the fourth floor of the dormitory from eight to eleven.

（女）　萬一你改變心意，我們八點到十一點間會在宿舍四樓的讀書室。

What is the man planning to do this evening？

男子今晚打算做什麼？

A.　Study for a final exam.

A.　準備期末考

B.　Visit friends in the dormitory.

B.　拜訪宿舍友人

C.　Work on an important paper.

C.　撰寫重要的報告

D.　Attend an economics class.

D.　出席經濟學課

正解　Ⓒ

本題情境是學校生活。對話以一個問句開始，故仔細聆聽說話者的回覆內容，就能掌握此段對話的重點訊息。

題目問男生今晚的計畫。對話中，女生詢問男生是否參加今天晚上讀書會的聚會，男生回答 I don't think so，意思即是 I don't think I am coming to your study group meeting.（我不想參加讀書會。）原因是：I've got to finish drafting my economics report before Tuesday. I want to concentrate on that first.（我必須在星期二前完成經濟學報告的初稿。我要先專心完成那個）。由此可知男生今天晚上要努力完成報告初稿，正解為 C。

關鍵字詞　draft 起草（文件、計畫）

第 13 題

(W) Look, over there. Do you see the tall white one with the black head?

(M) No. Hand me the binoculars.

(W) It's in the water at the edge of the pond.

(M) Oh, I see it now. Its beak is quite long and curved.

(W) Do you recognize the species?

(M) I'm not familiar with it. You'd better take a photo so we can identify it later.

（女）看，在那裡。你有看到高高白白、黑頭那隻嗎？

（男）沒有。給我望遠鏡。

（女）牠在池塘邊緣的水中。

（男）喔！我看到了。牠的嘴又長又彎。

（女）你認得牠的品種嗎？

（男）我不太熟悉這個品種。你最好照張相，我們晚點才能辨認。

What are the speakers doing?

A. Following a large animal's footprints.

B. Observing a creature from a distance.

C. Making a quick sketch in the wild.

D. Chasing a rare insect in the woods.

說話者正在做什麼？

A. 跟著一隻龐大動物的足跡

B. 遠距離觀察一種生物

C. 在野外素描

D. 在叢林裡追一隻稀有的昆蟲

正解 B

本題情境取材自賞鳥、觀察自然的活動。答題線索分布於整篇對話，必須整合關鍵字詞、理解關鍵詞與情境的關聯，才能正確推論出答案。

從對話可知，說話者正在自然環境中觀看某種動物，不過四個選項都是類似的情境，因此還必須掌握 binoculars、pond、beak、take a photo 這些關鍵字詞的意義。說話者手持「望遠鏡」、「相機」，附近有「池塘」。從 beak 一字可以確定說話者觀察的動物為「鳥類」。串聯這些關鍵字後可得知說話者是從遠距離觀察水鳥，故選項 B 是正解。

說話者沒有提到足跡，且選項 A 提到的 a large animal（龐大動物）並不符合我們對鳥類的描述；對話中沒有出現與素描相關的字詞，故選項 C 也不正確，而說話者是利用望遠鏡觀察，因此選項 D 也不是最適合的答案。

關鍵字詞 binoculars 望遠鏡　beak（鳥類的）嘴、喙

(W) Bill, I'm calling about the question you asked at the meeting today.

(M) Oh, about whether the cost analysis would be done by the end of this week.

(W) Yes, that's right. It looks like we'll have it for you on Friday.

(M) That's great. I'd like to review it over the weekend, before my business trip.

(W) You're leaving on Monday, right?

(M) Actually, I'm leaving Sunday evening.

（女） Bill，我打電話來是想和你談談今天你在會議上問的問題。

（男） 喔，你是說成本分析能不能在這週內完成嗎？

（女） 是的，沒錯。我們應該週五就能給你。

（男） 太好了。我想在週末先看過，在我出差之前。

（女） 你是下週一出發，對吧？

（男） 其實我是週日傍晚出發。

Why does Bill need the report this week?

A. He's leaving on Friday.

B. He needs to revise it.

C. He asked for it last week.

D. He'll be gone next week.

為什麼 Bill 這週就需要這份報告？

A. 他週五就要出發。

B. 他需要修改它。

C. 他上禮拜就要了。

D. 他下禮拜不在。

正解 D

本題為職場相關的情境。需運用整合歸納多項訊息的能力來理解對話的重要訊息，特別是與「時間」有關的資訊。

題目問「為什麼 Bill 這週就需要這份報告？」。Bill 希望在出差前先看過報告（I'd like to review it over the weekend, before my business trip）。另外一個資訊告訴我們 Actually, I'm leaving Sunday evening.（他星期天傍晚就出發了）。如果下禮拜報告才完成，Bill 就不在辦公室了，正確答案為 D。

關鍵字詞 analysis 分析

第 15 題

(W) Isn't this a tourist town?	（女）這裡不是觀光小鎮嗎？
(M) It was at one time, but hardly anyone visits it anymore.	（男）它曾經是，但是現在幾乎沒有人會造訪這裡了。
(W) Why is that?	（女）為什麼呢？
(M) The main highway used to go through the town. So people would stop along their way to have lunch or visit the shops. But then, the bypass was built. Now, few tourists stop.	（男）以前主要的高速公路會經過這裡。所以大家會在沿路的餐廳用餐或購物。不過外環道路已經完工了，現在很少旅客會在這停留了。
(W) Because they're eager to get to their destinations.	（女）因為他們想趕快到達目的地。
(M) Exactly.	（男）沒錯。

Why have tourists stopped visiting the town?	旅客為什麼不再造訪這個小鎮呢？
A. Because of unpleasant surroundings.	A. 因為附近環境欠佳
B. Because of a new road.	B. 因為一條新的道路
C. Because of a strict law.	C. 因為嚴格的法律
D. Because of overpriced parking.	D. 因為停車收費過高

正解 Ⓑ

本題取材自旅遊時發生的對話。需釐清上下文關係來理解對話，只要掌握對話中正確的前因後果，應該不難找到正解。

題目問為什麼旅客現在都不來這個小鎮。男生說明過去因為有公路通過，旅客們會在此用餐購物，接著說，But then, the bypass was built. Now, few tourists stop.（因為外環道路已經完工了，現在很少旅客會在這停留），因此選項 B 是最適合的答案。部份考生因為聽到 highway、lunch、shopping，誤以為這些字詞代表的是當地的環境而選了 A，忽略了對話中重要的因果線索。

關 鍵 字 詞 bypass 外環道路

(M) If I'm not mistaken, Frank has taken more sick leave than any other employee.

(W) It's true. I got a report from personnel last week about this very matter.

(M) Have you spoken to Frank about it yet?

(W) Not yet. I'm considering how to bring it up without embarrassing him.

(M) I favor the direct approach. After all, his job may be on the line.

(W) You may be right.

（男）如果我沒弄錯的話，Frank 請的病假比其他員工來的多。

（女）是這樣沒錯。上星期我收到人事部門針對這件事的報告。

（男）你找 Frank 聊過了嗎？

（女）還沒。我還在思考要如何在不讓他感到尷尬的情況下提出這件事。

（男）我喜歡直接一點的方式。畢竟，他的工作可能岌岌可危了。

（女）或許你說的對。

What are the two speakers mainly discussing?

A. A sick leave notice.

B. Frank's health problems.

C. The best way to approach Frank.

D. The reasons for Frank's absences.

這兩個人正在討論什麼？

A. 病假通知

B. Frank 的健康問題

C. 找 Frank 談話的最佳方式

D. Frank 缺席的理由

正解 C

本題情境取材自職場上的人事管理。仔細聽完對話，理解訊息之間的關係，才能做出正確的判斷。

題目問說話者正在討論什麼。部份考生聽到對話一開始的「Frank 請太多假」，便選擇了 D：Frank 缺席的理由。如果耐心把對話聽完，可以知道女生希望能夠在不讓 Frank 感到尷尬的情況下跟 Frank 談請假的事，而男生認為直接一點比較好，這兩個資訊都與如何找 Frank 聊聊的方法有關，因此正確答案為 C。

關鍵字詞 personnel 人事部門 approach 方法、態度

第 17 題

(M)	When will Bob and Alice arrive for lunch?
(W)	At 12:00, and they're bringing their son along.
(M)	How old is he?
(W)	Two, and he's very active.
(M)	In that case, we'd better put everything fragile out of his reach.
(W)	Like the antique vase on the table?
(M)	That's right. I'll put it in the closet right now.

（男）	Bob 和 Alice 今天什麼時候來午餐？
（女）	中午 12 點，他們會帶他們的兒子一起來。
（男）	他年紀多大？
（女）	兩歲，而且非常好動。
（男）	那樣的話，我們最好把易碎品放在他拿不到的地方。
（女）	例如桌上的那個古董花瓶？
（男）	沒錯。我現在就把它收到櫃子裡。

What are these people concerned about?

A. They have no time to clean up the house.
B. They haven't begun preparing lunch for their guests.
C. One of their family members may not come.
D. The little boy might damage something.

說話者正在擔憂什麼事？

A. 他們沒有時間整理家裡。
B. 他們還沒開始替客人準備午餐。
C. 其中一位家庭成員無法參加。
D. 那位小男孩可能會打破東西。

正解 Ⓓ

本題情境取材自家庭日常對話，需綜合對話上下文線索並根據語境推敲含意。

對話中的男生和女生今天有訪客 Bob 和 Alice，他們兩歲的兒子也會一同前來。女生告訴男生這個小孩非常好動（**very active**），男生便表示最好不要讓他接觸到易碎的物品，隨後他們的共識為先將古董花瓶收起來。由此可以推測，這兩個人擔憂小男孩可能會打破東西，正確答案是選項 **D**。

關鍵字詞 out of one's reach （使某人）接觸不到

第 18 題

(W) David, you seem very tired. Didn't you get enough sleep?	（女）David，你看起來很累。你沒有睡飽嗎？
(M) No, I got plenty of sleep. It's this medicine I'm taking for my cold. There's something in it that makes me feel really drowsy.	（男）不，我睡得很飽。是我吃的感冒藥。裡頭有成分讓我昏昏欲睡。
(W) Perhaps a cup of coffee would help you stay awake.	（女）或許喝杯咖啡可以讓你清醒一點。
(M) I've already had two cups of coffee today.	（男）我今天已經喝兩杯了。

What is David suffering from?

A. Sleep problems caused by stress.

B. A lack of nutrition.

C. An unpleasant side effect.

D. Anxiety about the future.

David 正在為了什麼感到苦惱？

A. 壓力導致的睡眠問題

B. 營養不良

C. 令人不舒服的副作用

D. 對未來的焦慮

正解 Ⓒ

本題內容取材自日常對話。需釐清上下文的關係來掌握重要的細節，對話一開始女生詢問男生為何看起來疲倦，需注意男生回答的原因。

對話中男生說他有睡飽，但是他為了治療感冒所吃的藥品中有成分讓他昏昏欲睡（It's this medicine I'm taking for my cold. There's something in it that makes me feel really drowsy.），所以他才會看起來很疲累。如果有掌握到對話中的 medicine、for my cold、makes me feel drowsy 這些關鍵字，就可以得知男生正在為藥物所產生的副作用而苦惱，因此正確答案為 C。

關鍵字詞 drowsy 昏昏欲睡 side effect 副作用

第 19 題

(W)	Patricia Hawkins just called.
(M)	Is she ready to meet with us?
(W)	Yes, she's finished a space plan for our living room. She also has some pictures of furniture selections she'd like to propose.
(M)	Good. When can we meet?
(W)	She suggested Saturday morning at ten.
(M)	That's fine with me.
(W)	OK, I'll let her know.

Who is the woman going to call?

A.　A land developer.

B.　A senior colleague.

C.　An art dealer.

D.　An interior designer.

（女）	Patricia Hawkins 剛剛來電。
（男）	她可以跟我們約見面了嗎？
（女）	對，她完成了我們客廳的設計圖。她還準備了一些建議的家具種類的照片。
（男）	好。我們什麼時候能跟她見面？
（女）	她提議星期六上午十點。
（男）	這時間我可以。
（女）	好，我再告訴她。

這個女生要打電話的對象是誰？

A.　土地開發商

B.　資深同事

C.　藝術品經銷商

D.　室內設計師

正解 Ⓓ

本題情境取材自居家生活。需根據少數句子的字面意義理解言談，最重要的是聽懂關鍵字詞。

題目問「這個女生要打電話的對象是誰？」，對話中沒有直接提到職稱或是身分，因此需要從人物所做的事判斷，女生提到 Yes, she's finished a space plan for our living room. She also has some pictures of furniture selections she'd like to propose. 得知該對象「完成了**空間設計**」、「有些建議的**家具**照片」，從這些關鍵句歸納出可以完成這些動作的人物，因此選項 D：An interior designer（室內設計師）是最適合的答案。如果只有聽到單一關鍵字 picture，可能會誤選 C；或只聽到 space plan，可能會誤選 A。

關鍵字詞　interior 內部的

Questions number 20 and 21 are based on the following conversation.

(M) That's the book you got at the airport?

(W) Yes. It's about the legendary actor Cary Grant. It's not the sort of thing I normally read.

(M) You usually bring mysteries on our diving trips.

(W) I didn't see any that caught my interest.

(M) A lot has already been written about Cary Grant. Does the author have anything new to offer?

(W) In fact, I've only read the first couple of chapters, and they mostly deal with his unhappy upbringing. His mother was hospitalized with depression.

(M) How did he get into entertainment?

(W) Believe it or not, he started out working in a circus, and later worked the lights for a magician.

(M) Maybe I'll look at it after you're finished.

第 20 題與第 21 題，請聽以下對話。

（男） 這就是你在機場買的書？

（女） 對啊，它是關於那個傳奇演員 Cary Grant。我平常其實不看這類書籍。

（男） 我們去潛水時，你通常都是帶懸疑小說。

（女） （在機場）我沒看到我有興趣的書。

（男） 有關 Cary Grant 的書相當多。這個作者有什麼新的內容嗎？

（女） 其實我才看了前面幾個章節而已，大多是跟他不愉快的童年有關。他母親因為憂鬱症接受治療。

（男） 他如何涉足演藝圈的呢？

（女） 信不信由你，他一開始是在馬戲團工作，接著擔任一位魔術師的燈光師。

（男） 等你讀完後，或許我也來讀一下。

第 20 題

Which type of book are the speakers discussing?

A. A biography.

B. A mystery.

C. A romance.

D. A travel guide.

說話者正在討論哪一類書籍？

A. 自傳

B. 懸疑小說

C. 浪漫小說

D. 旅遊指南

正解 Ⓐ

本題為一般社交情境，需整合歸納對話中的多項訊息，才能理解說話者談論的書籍類型。

對話中的幾項關鍵資訊包含：這本書是有關傳奇演員 Cary Grant、前幾章講述的是他的童年、他踏入演藝圈的契機，這些都是 Cary Grant 的生平事蹟，比較四個選項的書籍類型後，可知選項 A：A biography.（自傳）是最適合的答案。

答題時可能會因為聽到 mysteries 而誤選選項 B。男生在對話中表示「我們去潛水時，你通常都是帶懸疑小說。」其實，這是因為女生沒有在機場找到令她感興趣的懸疑小說（I didn't see any that caught my interest.），因此才買了一本她不常閱讀的書籍類型。如果有留意上下文的關聯，便能夠排除選項 B。

關鍵字詞　deal with 與…相關、處理　upbringing 養育、教養

What does the man imply about the woman's book?

A. He'll send it in a package.

B. He'll write a review of it.

C. He'll share it with someone else.

D. He'll consider reading it.

關於女生買的書，男生表示什麼意見？

A. 他將用包裹寄出。

B. 他會寫一篇書評。

C. 他將與其他人分享。

D. 他會考慮閱讀它。

正解 D

本題需根據對話中字面的意義理解言談。

聽完女生分享 Cary Grant 曾在馬戲團工作後，男生便說 Maybe I'll look at it after you're finished. 這句話的代名詞 it 指的就是他們在討論的這本書，男生的意思是「等你讀完後，或許我也來讀一下」，因此選項 D：He'll consider reading it（他會考慮閱讀這本書）是本題的正確答案。

關 鍵 字 詞 consider 考慮 (做某事)

第 22-23 題

Questions number 22 and 23 are based on the following conversation.

(W) Carson, how are you? It's good to see you again.

(M) Helena, I was hoping to see you here. Are you just arriving?

(W) Yes, I got a late start this morning. I missed the opening remarks and half of the plenary speech. I was sitting in the back. I didn't want to disturb anyone by coming to the front while the speaker was at the podium.

(M) You know, I've been thinking of sending you an email about a paper we might collaborate on.

(W) Really? I'd love to hear more. I need to publish something this year, but I haven't found a suitable topic to work on.

(M) Then this is a great opportunity. Shall we discuss it over lunch?

(W) Absolutely.

第 22 題與第 23 題，請聽以下對話。

（女） Carson，你好嗎？真開心又見到你。

（男） Helena，我正想在這見到你呢。你剛到嗎？

（女） 是的，我今天早上比較晚到。我錯過了開場致詞和一半的全體演講。我剛坐在後面。講者在講台上發表了，我不希望跑到前面打擾別人。

（男） 你知道嗎？我一直想寄封 email 給你，討論一篇我們可以合作的論文。

（女） 真的嗎？我很有興趣。我今年必須發表論文，但是我還沒有找到一個適合的主題。

（男） 那麼這會是個很棒的機會。要不要一起午餐順便討論一下呢？

（女） 當然好！

Where are the speakers?

A.　At a school reunion.

B.　At an outdoor concert.

C.　At a religious ceremony.

D.　At an academic conference.

說話者在哪裡？

A.　在同學會

B.　在戶外演唱會

C.　在宗教儀式中

D.　在學術研討會

正解　Ⓓ

本題取材自學術相關情境。綜合上下文的線索，根據對話中的關鍵字，推論對話可能發生的場合。

對話中出現數個重要的關鍵字，首先女生提到她錯過了開場致詞（opening remark）與全體演講（plenary speech）的前半部、而且不願意打擾講者（speaker）和專心聽講的聽眾，男生提到有個可以與女生合作寫論文（paper）的機會，並且從女生的回應，我們得知她有發表（publish）論文的壓力，整合這幾個關鍵字詞的關聯，可以推論說話的兩人應該是在學術界工作，因此選項 D 是最有可能的答案。

關鍵字詞　plenary speech（全體出席的）演講　podium 講台

第 23 題

Why was the man looking forward to talking with the woman?

男生為什麼期待與女生討論？

A. He hoped she could fulfill a promise.

A. 他希望她可以實現諾言。

B. He needs information from a speech he missed.

B. 他需要他錯過的演講資訊。

C. He has a proposal to make to her.

C. 他有個研究計畫想和她討論。

D. He wanted her to attend an event.

D. 他希望她能參加一場活動。

正解 C

本題需了解對話的脈絡，掌握上下文的因果關係即可正確地理解對話內容。

題目問的是男生期待與女生討論的原因。在這個對話中，與「期待討論」有關的訊息分別出現在兩處：第一次是男生見到女生打招呼時說道 I was hoping to see you here.（我正想在這見到你呢。）；第二次則出現在聽完女生解釋自己遲到而坐在後方後，男生接著說明希望能在這見到女生的原因是想跟她討論一篇可以合作的論文（You know, I've been thinking of sending you an email about a paper we might collaborate on.）。由此可知，男生期待的原因是因為他有個研究計畫想和女生討論。

關鍵字詞　collaborate 合作

Candidate	Department	Experience
Charles Lee	Law	Student representative
Susan Kim	History	None
Dennis Walter	Medicine	Candidate in 55th and 56th elections
Eric Morgan	Sociology	Current president of Student Union

候選人	系所	經歷
Charles Lee	法律	學生代表
Susan Kim	歷史	無
Dennis Walter	醫學	第 55 屆與第 56 屆候選人
Eric Morgan	社會學	現任學生會會長

第 25 題

For question number 24, please look at the table.

(W) Tomorrow we'll vote for the president of the student union, but I still haven't decided who I'll cast my ballot for.

(M) One of the candidates is from your department. Aren't you going to support her?

(W) Susan? No. She's just a freshman. I don't think she could handle the issues that are going on in the university.

(M) I supported the candidate from the Department of Medicine the past two years, but he has never been elected. I think I'll vote for someone else this time, maybe the guy from the law department. His record of standing up for student interests in meetings with school governors really impresses me.

(W) What about the current president? He's popular.

(M) Well, his close connection with the university's board of directors concerns me.

Which candidate will the man most likely vote for in the election?

A. Charles Lee.

B. Susan Kim.

C. Dennis Walter.

D. Eric Morgan.

第 24 題，請看表格。

（女）明天我們要投票選出學生會會長，但我還沒決定我要投票給誰。

（男）有一位候選人是你們系所的。你不支持她嗎？

（女）Susan 嗎？不，她才大一而已。我不認為她能處理大學裡的種種事務。

（男）過去兩年我都支持那位醫學院的候選人，但他從沒選上過。我想這次我會投給別人，或許法律系的那位。他在學校會議中捍衛學生權益的事蹟，令我印象深刻。

（女）現任會長如何呢？他很受歡迎。

（男）嗯，他跟大學董事會成員的關係密切令我擔憂。

男生最有可能在這次選舉投票給誰？

A. Charles Lee.

B. Susan Kim.

C. Dennis Walter.

D. Eric Morgan.

本題取材自校園情境，兩位說話者分享自己對於學生會長參選者的看法。聆聽對話時，需要整合聽到的線索和表格的資訊，才能理解、整理出對話者的立場。

題目問的是男生最有可能會投票給哪一位候選人。從男生的回答，我們可以得知過去兩年他都支持醫學院的候選人（I supported the candidate from the Department of Medicine the past two years.），但這位候選人從沒選上過，聽的時候需留意對話中的時態，以免誤解。他說 I think I'll vote for someone else this time, maybe the guy from the law department.（我想這次我會投給別人，或許是法律系的那位。）接著他說明選擇投給法律系候選人的原因。對照表格，我們可以確定法律系的候選人指的便是選項 A：Charles Lee。

分析比較類的圖表題訊息較多、較複雜，可利用前方提到的筆記分類法來歸納訊息，以本題為例，可邊聽邊將訊息整理如下表，會更容易更有系統地掌握語意。

Candidate	Man	Woman
Charles Lee	He may vote for him.	
Susan Kim		She won't support her.
Dennis Walter	He voted for him the past two years.	
Eric Morgan	He has concerns.	

關 鍵 字 詞 ballot 選票 board 董事會、委員會

第 25 題　New!

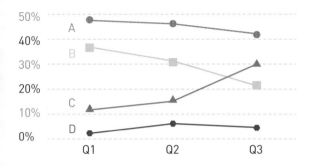

For question number 25, please look at the chart.	第 25 題，請看圖表。

(W)　As you can see from the chart, while Asia remained the major source of customers for our hotels, the percentage dropped in the last quarter.

（女）從圖表中可見，雖然亞洲依舊是我們旅館最大的客源，但是在上一季百分比下降了。

(M)　Wasn't that expected? We shifted more of our advertising budget to North America and Europe.

（男）這難道不是我們意料中的嗎？我們把較多的廣告預算移到北美與歐洲。

(W)　Yes, but the proportion of reservations made in the U.S. and Canada actually declined sharply, while the share in Europe increased greatly.

（女）是的，但是美國與加拿大的訂房率卻大幅下滑，歐洲的比例則有明顯成長。

(M)　So we need to figure out why North American guests were staying away.

（男）所以我們需要了解為什麼北美的顧客持續流失中。

Which line in the chart refers to North American guests?

圖表中的哪一條線代表北美的顧客？

A.　Line A.

B.　Line B.

C.　Line C.

D.　Line D.

A.　A 線

B.　B 線

C.　C 線

D.　D 線

本題取材自旅館業者的市場分析。要掌握完整資訊，對話和圖表的訊息缺一不可，聆聽對話的內容時，應同時搭配圖表資訊。

根據對話，我們可知亞洲客人比例在上一季雖有下滑，但仍是主要客群，占全體比例最高的 A 線應該代表亞洲客源。相對之下 the proportion of reservations made in the U.S. and Canada actually declined sharply（美國與加拿大的訂房比率卻大幅下降），對照圖表後只有 B 線呈現大幅下降的趨勢，因此合理判斷 B 線代表北美客群。歐洲的客人則是明顯增加（the share in Europe increased greatly），因此 C 線代表歐洲顧客，而對話中未提到 D 線的相關資訊。將對話資訊與圖表結合後，可得知正確答案為 B。

關鍵字詞 share 一份、部份

🔍 關鍵字詞

接著我們來複習本部份的重點詞彙

tease 　**動**　戲弄、取笑（第 11 題）

例句　• You're teasing me.
　　　　你在逗我吧。

　　　• Mary's colleagues teased her about her new hair color, so she has decided to dye her hair again tonight.
　　　　Mary 的同事嘲笑她的新髮色，所以她決定今晚重染。

amateur 　**名**　業餘從事者、外行（第 11 題）

例句　• The woman is an experienced amateur painter.
　　　　這位女子是個經驗豐富的業餘畫家。

　　　• The amateur director competed in the city film festival, and his clip outperformed many works created by professionals.
　　　　這位業餘導演參加城市電影節的競選，他的作品勝過許多專業導演創作的電影。

draft 　**動**　起草（文件、計畫）（第 12 題）

例句　• I've got to finish drafting my economics report before Tuesday.
　　　　我必須在星期二前完成經濟學報告的初稿。

　　　• Before starting the new project, the construction company drafted a proposal to the city government.
　　　　新建案開始之前，這家建設公司起草一份計畫書提交給市政府。

binoculars 　**名**　望遠鏡（第 13 題）

例句　• Hand me the binoculars.
　　　　給我望遠鏡。

　　　• Through binoculars, even the audience in the back rows can observe the subtle changes in performers' facial expressions.
　　　　透過望遠鏡，即使是坐在後排的觀眾也可以觀察到演出者表情的細微變化。

beak 名 （鳥類的）嘴、喙（第 13 題）

例句 • Its beak is quite long and curved.
牠的嘴又長又彎。

• A chicken uses its beak to peck at seeds on the ground.
一隻小雞用嘴啄食地上的種子。

analysis 名 分析（第 14 題）

例句 • I'm calling to ask about whether the cost analysis would be done by the end of this week.
我打電話來詢問，成本分析能不能在這週內完成。

• Both sufficient data and a reasonable theoretical framework are essential to completing a valid analysis.
充足的資料和合理的理論架構是完成有效分析的必要條件。

bypass 名 外環道路（第 15 題）

例句 • But then, the bypass was built. Now, few tourists stop.
不過外環道路已經完工了，現在很少旅客會在這停留了。

• To avoid traffic, the commuter takes the bypass rather than driving through the city center.
為了避免交通壅塞，開車通勤的人會走外環道路，不經過市中心。

personnel 名 人事部門（第 16 題）

例句 • I got a report from personnel last week about this very matter.
上星期我收到人事部門針對這件事的報告。

• The personnel officer is in charge of recruiting staff and negotiating employment contracts.
人事專員負責聘僱員工和協議聘雇合約。

approach 名 方法、態度（第 16 題）

例句 • I favor the direct approach.
我喜歡直接一點的方式。

- The lecturer altered his approach to teaching literature by encouraging students to read out loud.
  這位講師將他教授文學的方式改為鼓勵學生朗讀。

out of one's reach （使某人）接觸不到（第 17 題）

例句
- In that case, we'd better put everything fragile out of his reach.
  那樣的話，我們最好把易碎物品放在他拿不到的地方。

- Though the goal seems out of her reach, she insists on registering for the marathon.
  雖然這個目標看似遙不可及，她仍堅持報名馬拉松。

drowsy 形 昏昏欲睡（第 18 題）

例句
- There's something in this medicine that makes me feel really drowsy.
  這藥裡頭有成分讓我昏昏欲睡。

- People taking sleep medication at night feel drowsy even during daytime.
  晚上服用安眠藥的人即使在白天也會感到昏昏欲睡。

side effect 名 副作用（第 18 題）

例句
- David is suffering from an unpleasant side effect.
  David 有很不舒服的副作用。

- The side effects of prescription drugs are listed on the label so that consumers can recognize the symptoms.
  處方用藥的副作用列在標籤上，方便服用者辨認症狀。

interior 形 內部的（第 19 題）

例句
- The woman is going to call her interior designer.
  這個女生要打電話給她的室內設計師。

- Rather than extravagant decorations, the interior design utilizes natural ventilation and sufficient lighting.
  室內設計應運用自然通風和充足的採光，而非浮誇的裝飾。

deal with 與…相關、處理（第 20 題）

例句
- In fact, I've only read the first couple of chapters, and they mostly deal with his unhappy upbringing.
  其實我才看了前面幾個章節而已，大多是跟他不愉快的童年有關。

- The actor deals with stage fright by pausing briefly before saying his first line.
  這位演員在說第一句台詞前稍作停頓，以克服怯場。

upbringing 名 養育、教養（第 20 題）

例句
- The method of upbringing in one's childhood influences the values and attitudes of a lifetime.
  兒童時期的養育方式影響人一生的價值觀和態度。

consider 動 考慮（做某事）（第 21 題）

例句
- He'll consider reading it.
  他會考慮閱讀它。

- The company is considering adding a new product line, but they haven't made the final decision yet.
  這家公司正在考慮增加一條新的生產線，但是還沒做最後的決定。

plenary speech 名 （全體出席的）演講（第 22 題）

例句
- I missed the opening remarks and half of the plenary speech.
  我錯過了開場致詞和一半的全體演講。

- The professor will give a plenary speech at the end of the conference, so other sessions should be finished before then.
  這位教授在研討會結束前有一場全體演講，所以其他場次要在這之前結束。

podium 名 講台（第 22 題）

例句
- I didn't want to disturb anyone by coming to the front while the speaker was at the podium.
  講者在講台上發表了，我不希望跑到前面打擾別人。

- Standing at the podium in front of the lecture hall is today's invited speaker.
  站在講堂前方講台上的是今天的受邀講者。

collaborate 動 合作（第 23 題）

例句
- I've been thinking of sending you an email about a paper we might collaborate on.
  我一直想寄封 email 給你，討論一篇我們可以合作的論文。

- The state government and a contractor are collaborating on an undersea tunnel connecting the capital and a nearby island.
  州政府和一家承包商正在合作建造連接首府和鄰島的一座海底隧道。

延伸學習 collaborate <u>on</u> something; collaborate <u>in doing</u> something 合作某事

ballot 名 選票（第 24 題）

例句
- Tomorrow we'll vote for the president of the student union, but I still haven't decided who I'll cast my ballot for.
  明天我們要投票選出學生會會長，但我還沒決定我要投票給誰。

- British voters cast ballots to express their opinion on leaving the European Union.
  英國人民投票表達對於脫歐的意見。

延伸學習 cast a ballot 投票

board 名 董事會、委員會（第 24 題）

例句
- His close connection with the university's board of directors concerns me.
  他跟大學董事會成員的關係密切令我擔憂。

- As the term of service at the literature association will end soon, a board meeting was held to elect the next chairperson.
  因為文學協會理事長的任期即將結束，委員開會選出下一任理事長。

share 名 一份、部份（第 25 題）

例句
- The proportion of reservations made in the U.S. and Canada actually declined sharply while the share in Europe increased greatly.
  美國與加拿大的訂房率大幅下滑，歐洲的比例則有明顯成長。

- Before my share of work is done, I cannot be distracted by other tasks.
  在完成我的工作之前，我不能受到其他事干擾。

1. 加強理解言外之意的能力

有時候說話者會採取較迂迴或委婉的語言策略，例如：The company had a very humble beginning.（這家公司在草創初期非常艱辛），此處的 humble 不是謙虛的意思，而是指資源匱乏而艱辛。平常學習時如果遇到不熟悉、不是一般字面上意義的詞彙，記得將意思記下、增加印象；也可以多練習猜測、判斷訊息間的關聯，推論字面以外的意思，語言互動與溝通表達的能力才能更上層樓。

2. 養成預期的能力（prediction）

培養推理與後設思考（例如預測）的能力也是英語聽力素養重要的一環。可以從對話的第一句話判斷對話的情境，接著預想接下去可能會聽到什麼訊息。一旦新出現的訊息與預想的不同，要迅速調整修正，和前面已聽到的訊息整合。

3. 多接觸英語媒體，累積詞彙

平時應主動探索課外相關資訊，擴展英語文學習場域，並運用各種資源強化自主學習，例如閱讀英文報章雜誌、小說、或是收聽英語新聞或看英文電影、影集，自然地累積與時事及流行話題相關的詞彙及用語。

4. 整合聽到與看到的資訊

生活中，大部分時候我們都是同時運用聽覺與視覺來接收外界的資訊，例如收看電視節目、聆聽課堂演說等，單純使用聽覺接收訊息的情況反而較少。因此，圖表題的設計是符合日常英語的使用，與核心素養所強調的情境化、生活化原則一致。建議學習者平時可利用網路資源，尋找搭配圖表的簡短影音片段，先用幾秒鐘迅速瀏覽圖表重點，例如是關於金額、地點或人名，預測可能的問題，再仔細聆聽對話內容尋找關鍵線索。平時習慣視覺和聽覺雙管齊下，讓注意力可以延伸得更廣，才是提升聽力理解與溝通能力的不二法門。

Note

TALKS

中高級聽力
第三部份

談話

 聽力測驗
第三部份 談 話

這部份每題有一段談話,搭配 2-3 個問題,須先正確理解談話內容,再根據問題,選出正確的答案。

本部份評量的學習表現包括:

✓ 能聽懂英語談話
★ 能聽懂情節發展及細節描述
★ 能根據上下文釐清訊息
★ 能分析、歸納多項訊息
★ 能綜合相關資訊預測可能的發展或做合理猜測
★ 能理解說話者的觀點、態度與言外之意

考前提醒

這個部份主要評量考生是否理解各類型的談話,以及整合歸納重點的能力。評量的談話種類包含一般的演講、報導、電話留言、宣布事項、廣播節目、廣告、簡報、討論及操作說明等。內容情境多與日常生活、學校生活及工作場合相關。

除了前一單元提到的聽解方式外,作答時,還可運用以下幾個方法幫助理解:

1. 留意播音提到的談話種類

每段談話播出之前,會有談話種類的提示,例如:announcement、radio program、lecture 等,請仔細聽清楚,預先了解談話的類型,對了解談話情境有相當大的幫助。

2. 聆聽題目、筆記重點資訊

筆記的方式建議為記下主要概念和重要的舉例，而不是把聽到的全部寫下來，因為時間會不夠。另外，如果聽到新的或是較陌生的概念，可先記下關鍵字，並留意之後是否有進一步的解釋。

3. 多留意關鍵資訊

聆聽談話前先看選項或圖表，可以幫助判斷答題需要的關鍵資訊。另外，開場和總結都要全神貫注聆聽，例如第 28-29 題說話者一開始就開門見山說出此留言的主要目的。聽到總結性詞語 To sum up、To conclude 時也需特別注意，因為之後會接著結論或是再次強調重點資訊，可以確認自己理解的主題和重點是否正確。

4. 釐清代名詞指涉的對象

通常代名詞的出現會指涉一個剛剛提到不久的名詞，尚且需要從語意確認。例如 The well-known enterprise was invited to provide internship opportunities. （這家知名企業受邀提供實習機會）Many students took advantage of them to practice what was taught in school. （很多學生藉此練習學校所教過的知識）此處 them 指涉的對象需要從前面提過的名詞找，因為是複數形，可能的選擇只有 many students 和上一句的 opportunities，接著確認語意為「利用實習機會」，所以 them 在這裡指涉 opportunities。釐清指涉對象，才能夠了解正確的語意（例如第 27 題）。

5. 歸納談話的要點

選項中的字詞不一定會和談話內容用一模一樣的字彙與句型，所以需要練習歸納要點，再和選項比對，如此可以避免遺漏關鍵語意（例如第 30 題與 32 題）。

6. 留意轉折詞與時態，掌握談話的脈絡

較長篇的英文談話常會利用轉折詞（transition）讓內容更加清楚易懂，留意這些轉折詞可幫助理解上下文關係，掌握談話的脈絡。當說話者要補充說明時會使用 in addition、furthermore；若要呈現對比關係則多使用 however、on the other hand；說明因果或目的常使用 due to、as a result、in order to。最常見的則是表示順序的轉折詞，例如：first/second 等序數、then、finally 以及表示時間關係的連接詞，例如：as soon as、after、before 等。另外，英文的時態也是了解談話內容的重要線索，多留意時態才能正確掌握事件發生的時間。例如第 35-37 題與第 38-40 題，留意談話中的轉折詞以及時態，有助釐清訊息。

以上方法可以視不同題目的需求，選用適合的策略組合！

Questions number 26 and 27 are based on the following announcement.

Can I have your attention, everyone? Tomorrow, we're going to hike to the bottom of the Grand Canyon, where we'll camp overnight beside the Colorado River. The trail we're going to take is about eleven kilometers long, so the hike down will take us about three hours. Besides your camping gear, bring along at least three liters of water since there will be none available until we reach the campground. Now, tomorrow's hike will be much easier than the trip back up on Wednesday. That will take us about eight hours, so be prepared for a real workout. Are there any questions? If not, we'll meet back here at 6:00 A.M.

26 到 27 題

本段談話發生在旅遊時，說話者是領隊，他正在對團員解說明日的健行路線與行程，提醒他們需攜帶的物品、集合時間等注意事項。

What is the main purpose of this announcement?

A. To provide details about a planned activity.

B. To outline rules for using a campground.

C. To promote a tour of a national park.

D. To describe a trip down a dangerous river.

這段宣布事項的主要目的為何？

A. 提供已規劃的活動細節

B. 概述營地的規定

C. 推廣國家公園行程

D. 描述順著危險河流而下的一趟旅程

正解 Ⓐ

本題談話內容取材自旅遊時領隊對團員的宣布事項，需整合分散在談話中的多項資訊，才能得知此段談話的主要目的。

此段談話中，說話者先大致說明健行地點（we're going to hike to the bottom of the Grand Canyon），接著提供更多相關細節，例如：步道距離（The trail we're going to take is about eleven kilometers long.）、步行時間（the hike down will take us about three hours）、攜帶物品（Besides your camping gear, bring along at least three liters of water），最後提醒聽者集合時間（we'll meet back here at 6:00 A.M.），因此我們可以得知此段談話的主要目的為 To provide details about a planned activity.（提供已規劃的活動細節）。

關鍵字詞 gear 裝備

第 27 題

What does the speaker point out about the hike on Wednesday?

說話者提到關於週三健行的什麼事情？

A. It'll be interrupted by frequent rest stops.

B. It'll follow a circular route.

C. It'll be shorter than tomorrow's.

D. It'll be quite exhausting.

A. 它會被頻繁的休息中斷。

B. 它會沿著一條環形路線。

C. 它會比明天的路線短。

D. 它會非常累人。

本題需比較談話後半段所提到週三的健行與明天的行程，同時也要注意談話中所指涉對象。說話者提到 tomorrow's hike will be much easier than the trip back up on Wednesday. That will take us about eight hours, so be prepared for a real workout. （明天的健行會比週三的上坡路線更加容易。週三的路線須耗費約八小時，所以大家要準備好面對真正的鍛鍊）。此處，需注意 that 所指涉的對象為「週三的行程」而非「明日的行程」才不會產生誤解。另外，前面說話者提到 the hike down will take us about three hours.（下坡約需三小時），因此可得知週三的健行路線是比明日更累人的。說話者未提到「休息」或是「環狀路線」，因此選項 A 與 B 都不是正確答案。另外，週三與明日的路線差別在於上坡與下坡，未提到路線長短，因此選項 C 亦不正確。

關鍵字詞　**workout** 鍛鍊

第 28-29 題

Questions number 28 and 29 are based on the following telephone message.

Peter? This is Joan. You told me recently that you were interested in buying a used car. Well, I may have found the perfect one for you. It belongs to the German couple that live upstairs. They mentioned to me today that they'll be moving back to Germany soon and intend to sell their car. They bought it seven years ago but it's still in excellent condition, as they haven't driven it very far, only about 25,000 kilometers. It has a two-liter engine, seats five people comfortably, and they're asking NT$150,000, which is in your price range. If you're interested, I'll arrange a time when you can look at the car and test drive it. Bye.

28-29 題

本段談話是一則電話留言，Joan 告知 Peter 有關她鄰居要出售二手車的訊息。內容主要說明車主出售的原因、該輛車的狀況、里程數、排氣量與出售價錢等。

第 28 題

Why did the speaker leave this telephone message?

A. To suggest some repairs to Peter's car.

B. To inform Peter of a car that's for sale.

C. To list the advantages of a German car.

D. To give Peter the use of her car.

說話者為什麼留下這則電話留言？

A. 為 Peter 的車提出維修建議

B. 告知 Peter 一輛出售車輛的資訊

C. 列出德國車的優點

D. 同意 Peter 可開她的車

正解　B

本段談話為一則電話留言，只要理解關鍵句子的字面意義就可以得知這則留言的目的。

Joan 一開始提到 You told me recently that you were interested in buying a used car. Well, I may have found the perfect one for you. （你最近告訴我你想買一輛二手車，我幫你找到一輛最適合你的車了），因此我們可以得知這則留言的主要目的是要告知 Peter 關於這輛車的資訊，正確答案為 B。

關鍵字詞　intend 打算

第 29 題

What does the speaker imply about the car?

A. Some parts have recently been replaced.

B. The interior is very luxurious.

C. There's nothing seriously wrong with it.

D. It's a popular model.

關於這輛車，說話者暗示了什麼？

A. 部份零件近期已更換過。

B. 它的內裝非常豪華。

C. 它沒有重大瑕疵。

D. 它是很受歡迎的型號。

本題需根據談話中線索推敲含意，先掌握關鍵字詞，再根據隱含的線索推論。同時也要聽懂留言中其他重要細節，才能排除誘答選項。

Joan 在留言中提到 it's still in excellent condition（它的車況佳），所以我們可推論此輛車應該沒有重大瑕疵，故選項 B 為正解。另外，Joan 在留言中只提到出售原因（they'll be moving back to Germany）、里程數（25,000 kilometers）、排氣量（a two-liter engine）、乘坐人數（seats five people）、價錢（they're asking NT$150,000），並未提到零件、內裝或是型號，故其他選項非正確答案。

關鍵字詞 condition 狀況、狀態

第 30-31 題

Questions number 30 and 31 are based on the following lecture.

Every summer, the Wimbledon tennis championships take place in Britain. This three-week event is attended by half a million people. Years ago, the tournament also attracted hundreds of pigeons, which feasted on crumbs left behind by spectators. While looking for food, the pigeons would fly around the courts and dirty them with their droppings. One year, organizers hired Apex Control, which offered a brilliant solution. Apex Control uses hawks to keep pigeons away from airports and other sites. During the next Wimbledon tournament, a handler flew a hawk around the courts several times before matches began. That was enough to scare the pigeons away. Since then, the hawks have visited Wimbledon every summer. And the pigeons have ceased to be a problem.

30 到 31 題

本段談話為一段演說，說話者講述英國的溫布頓網球賽常有鴿子破壞場地整潔，主辦單位因此利用老鷹盤旋在上空以驅趕鴿子。

第 30 題

What were the event organizers most likely concerned about at the venue?

A. Poorly maintained seats.

B. Damage caused by spectators.

C. A threat to hygiene.

D. Inconsistent dimensions.

關於場地，主辦單位最有可能擔憂的是什麼？

A. 維護不善的座位

B. 觀眾造成的破壞

C. 衛生隱憂

D. 不一致的尺寸

正解 C

本段談話內容是一段關於溫布頓網球賽如何避免鴿子破壞場地的演說。需釐清上下文關係了解談話中的前因後果，才能正確理解整體大意。

說話者提到 the pigeons would fly around the courts and dirty them with their droppings.（鴿子會在球場四處飛行，而牠們的排泄物會弄髒場地），談話後半提到主辦單位利用老鷹驅趕鴿子，因此可推知主辦單位對於場地的擔憂主要來自鴿子。另外，需歸納談話主旨並試著換句話說，鴿子排泄物是衛生問題，因此選項 C 即為正確答案。其他選項都與鴿子或衛生無關，都不是正確答案。

關鍵字詞 tournament 錦標賽 droppings（鳥獸的）排泄物 hygiene 衛生

According to this lecture, what is used by Apex Control at various places?

根據此段演說，Apex Control 在各地使用哪一項工具？

A. Birds of prey.

B. Remote control aircraft.

C. Poisonous chemicals.

D. Radar transmitters.

A. 猛禽

B. 遙控飛機

C. 有毒化學物質

D. 雷達傳送器

正解 Ⓐ

本題需根據關鍵字詞的字面意義理解談話。

談話者提到 Apex Control uses hawks to keep pigeons away from airports and other sites.（Apex Control 在機場與其他地點利用老鷹來驅趕鴿子），而老鷹為一種猛禽，因此可得知正確答案為 A。

關鍵字詞 bird of prey 猛禽

第 32-34 題

Questions number 32 to 34 are based on the following talk.

If you have a garden, then you may want to consider tulips and other blooming plants that grow from bulbs. Generally speaking, the ideal time to plant bulbs is in the fall. Before you start, measure the area that you will plant. Accurate measurements can help you decide how many bulbs you should buy since each bulb type requires a different amount of space to thrive. Choose bulbs that reflect your preferences in terms of color, height, bloom time, and ability to grow in sun or shade. To ensure that the bulbs you choose will produce more blooms, select them carefully. Pick those that are free of bruises and soft spots. Later, when you're ready to plant, follow the instructions on the bulb package.

32 到 34 題

本段談話主要介紹球莖植物。說話者說明種植球莖植物時的注意事項，例如：種植時間、所需面積、如何挑選球莖等。

第 32 題

What does this talk mainly provide?

A. Benefits and drawbacks of bulbs.

B. A comparison of different types of bulbs.

C. Guidance on planting and purchasing bulbs.

D. An account of the popularity of bulbs.

此段談話主要提供了什麼訊息？

A. 球莖的優缺點

B. 不同種類球莖的比較

C. 種植與購買球莖的指引

D. 關於球莖受歡迎程度的說明

正解 Ⓒ

此段談話取材自一段說明種植球莖植物的演說。需整合分散在談話中的資訊，才能完整理解談話的主要大意。

說話者一開始提到 the ideal time to plant bulbs is in the fall（種植球莖植物最佳時間在秋天）、後半提到 Pick those that are free of bruises and soft spots.（挑選無碰傷與壓起來不會軟軟的球莖），以及 follow the instructions on the bulb package.（遵照球莖包裝上的說明），綜合以上線索，得知本段談話主要在說明種植與購買球莖的注意事項。

關鍵字詞 tulip 鬱金香　bulb 球莖　guidance 指引、指導

According to this talk, what should people know about the plot of land in which bulbs will be planted?

A. The fertility of the soil.

B. Its width and length.

C. The pests that breed in it.

D. Its proximity to water.

根據此段談話，種植球莖植物時人們應該知道關於土地的何事？

A. 土壤肥沃度

B. 寬度與長度

C. 在裡面繁衍的害蟲

D. 是否鄰近水源

正解 B

作答本題時，首先需掌握談話中關鍵句子與詞彙，接著推論與關鍵詞彙相關的同義字，建構出完整的語意，才能推論出正確答案。

說話者在談話中間提到 Before you start, measure the area that you will plant. Accurate measurements can help you decide how many bulbs you should buy since each bulb type requires a different amount of space to thrive.（開始前，先測量你要種植的面積大小。準確的測量可幫助你決定要購買多少球莖，因為每種球莖生長所需的空間不同。）因此可得知正解與「測量」相關，利用一般知識可推知測量土地時通常是測量寬度與長度，因此選項 B 為正確答案。

關鍵字詞 measurement 測量 thrive 茁壯

第 34 題

Which factor influences the number of blooms that a bulb will produce?

A. Its physical appearance.

B. Its origin.

C. Its smell.

D. Its moisture.

何項因素影響球莖植物的花朵數量？

A. 它的外觀

B. 它的原產地

C. 它的味道

D. 它的溼度

正解 A

本題需先理解關鍵字詞後才能做出推論。

說話者最後提到 To ensure that the bulbs you choose will produce more blooms, select them carefully. Pick those that are free of bruises and soft spots.（為確保你挑選的球莖會開更多的花，你要精挑細選。挑選無碰傷與壓起來不會軟軟的球莖。）可得知球莖是否有碰傷會影響開花數量，而這是由外觀可得知的，因此正確答案為 A。

關鍵字詞 bruise 碰傷、瘀傷

Room	Tasks	Done
12-A	Fix front door lock	✓
6-B	Handle noise complaint	✓
7-B	?	✗
9-A	Repair smoke alarm	✓

房號	事項	完成
12-A	修理門鎖	✓
6-B	處理噪音投訴	✓
7-B	?	✗
9-A	修理煙霧偵測器	✓

For questions number 35 to 37, please look at the progress report.

Hello, Mrs. Stuart. This is Matthew Morris. I've sent you a progress report on the issues you wanted me to look into. I took care of the problem with 12-A yesterday. The tenant's key got stuck in the lock, so we had a locksmith install a new lock. As for the complaint about a strange noise from the roof of 6-B, I haven't been able to get in touch with the tenant. I put a note in her mailbox, and I expect she will contact me when she returns. Then the tenant in 7-B gave me the rent he owed last night. Finally, I examined the smoke alarm in 9-A. There was nothing seriously wrong. The batteries just needed to be replaced.

35 到 37 題

本段談話是一則電話留言以及一張進度表。說話者正在留言給 Stuart 女士報告他需處理事項的工作進度。說話者針對此份進度表上的事項一一說明他的處理狀況。

第 35 題

Who is this message most likely intended for?

A. A real estate agent.

B. A fire safety inspector.

C. A prospective tenant.

D. A building manager.

這則留言最有可能是留給誰？

A. 房屋仲介

B. 消防安全檢查員

C. 未來的房客

D. 大樓管理經理

正解 **D**

本段談話取材自與社區住戶事務相關的一則留言。首先根據談話中的線索釐清說話者與聽者的關係與身分，並聽懂文中細節，做出推論，這麼做也可以排除誘答選項。

說話者一開始提到 I've sent you a progress report on the issues you wanted me to look into.（關於你要我處理的事項，我已經寄給妳一份進度表。），因此我們可得知聽者是需要掌握這些事項進度的人，接著聽下去得知說話者提到他處理的事務包含門鎖（The tenant's key got stuck in the lock）、噪音（the complaint about a strange noise from the roof of 6-B）、房租（the tenant in 7-B gave me the rent he owed）以及煙霧偵測器（I examined the smoke alarm in 9-A），最有可能需要了解這些事項處理進度的人應該是大樓管理經理，因此正確答案為 D。其他選項雖然與這些問題略有相關，但這些身分的人都不需處理住戶的所有問題。

本段留言因為涉及的細節較多，除了注意說話者提到的房號並對照進度表外，多留意談話中的轉折詞與時態，有助掌握談話的脈絡。例如說話者在留言中使用了 as for、then、finally 等轉折詞，聽到這些轉折詞時，可預期接下來說話者要講述的是另一個問題。另外，此留言中說話者大多使用過去式，但是提到 6-B 的投訴問題時使用的時態是否定的現在完成式，因此可推知他尚未解決 6-B 的投訴問題。多多留意這些轉折詞與時態，能幫助理解談話內容。

關鍵字詞 tenant 房客

第 36 題

Based on the message, which item should appear in the shaded area?

根據此留言，下列何項會出現在灰影處？

A. Collect overdue payment.
B. Identify source of leak.
C. Complete basic repairs.
D. Issue parking permit.

A. 收取過期費用
B. 找出漏水的原因
C. 完成基本維修
D. 發放停車證

本題需整合此段談話與進度表中的多項訊息。首先理解談話中的重要細節，再搭配進度表的資訊，就可推知灰影處的問題為何。

灰影處是房客 7-B 的問題，因此要特別留意說話者提到 7-B 的部份。談話中提到 Then the tenant in 7-B gave me the rent he owed last night. （7-B 的房客昨晚給我他積欠的房租），因此我們可得知正確答案為 A。

關鍵字詞 overdue 過期

第 37 題

What does the speaker imply about the problem in 9-A?

關於 9-A 的問題，說話者暗示了什麼？

A. Its cause has been identified.

A. 原因已經找到。

B. A technician has failed to arrive.

B. 技工無法前來。

C. Its consequences have been calculated.

C. 後果已經估算過。

D. A legal dispute has been settled.

D. 法律糾紛已經解決。

本題需根據談話中的脈絡進行詮釋，需聽懂關鍵句子並做出推論。

說話者提到 I examined the smoke alarm in 9-A. There was nothing seriously wrong. The batteries just needed to be replaced. （我檢查了 9-A 的煙霧偵測器，並沒有嚴重問題，只需更換電池。）因此我們可推知說話者已查明煙霧偵測器問題所在，故正確答案為 A。

關鍵字詞 smoke alarm 煙霧偵測器

第 38-40 題　　**New!**

Time	Paper Presentation	
	Speaker(s)	Location
1:10	Daniel Brown	Main Auditorium
2:30	Chuck Stein	South Hall
3:30	Julia Yeh	East Hall
4:30	Mary Robinson	Central Hall

時間	論文發表	
	講者	地點
1:10	Daniel Brown	大禮堂
2:30	Chuck Stein	南棟
3:30	Julia Yeh	東棟
4:30	Mary Robinson	中央棟

For questions number 38 to 40, please look at the agenda.

Welcome back. I've got two announcements. There have been several alterations to today's schedule. If you have today's program with you, I suggest you take notes. First, because of a problem with the air conditioning in East Hall, Ms. Julia Yeh's presentation scheduled to begin at 3:30 will be held in Central Hall instead. We apologize for the inconvenience, but your comfort is a priority. Next, there was an error in the program. Two speakers' names were switched. The upcoming presentation at 2:30 will be given by Dr. Mary Robinson, not Dr. Chuck Stein. All right. I appreciate everyone's patience, and now let's welcome the speaker of this session, Dr. Mary Robinson, to the stage.

38 到 40 題

本段談話發生在研討會，結合研討會議程表。說話者正在宣布兩項關於本日議程的變更。第一項是其中一位講者需更動論文發表地點，第二項是議程表有誤，兩位講者的姓名被調換。

What is the purpose of the speaker's first announcement?

A. To introduce a facility.

B. To praise two staff members.

C. To congratulate the organizer.

D. To explain a change.

說話者宣布第一項事項的目的為何？

A. 介紹一項設施

B. 表揚兩位工作人員

C. 恭賀主辦者

D. 說明變更

正解 D

作答本題時，需掌握談話中與順序相關的轉折詞（first、next）、釐清上下文關係，應該不難理解談話脈絡。

本題問的是第一項宣布事項，因此要特別留意談話中的一開始提到的事項或是有無提到 first 等字。說話者一開始提到 There have been several alterations to today's schedule.（今日的議程有幾項變動。）接著繼續說明 First, because of a problem with the air conditioning in East Hall, Ms. Julia Yeh's presentation scheduled to begin at 3:30 will be held in Central Hall instead.（首先，由於東棟的空調問題，Julia Yeh 預定於三點半發表的場次將移至中央棟。）我們可得知第一項宣布事項主要是要說明場地變更事宜，故正確答案為 D。

關鍵字詞 alteration 變更

第 39 題

Where is this announcement most likely being given? 　　　此宣布事項是在哪裡宣布的？

A. In Main Auditorium. 　　　A. 大禮堂

B. In South Hall. 　　　B. 南棟

C. In East Hall. 　　　C. 東棟

D. In Central Hall. 　　　D. 中央棟

正解 B

本題需整合歸納此段宣布事項與議程表的多項訊息，一邊聆聽說話者提供的資訊，一邊對照議程表修改，才能得知正確的資訊。

說話者提到 Next, there was an error in the program. Two speakers' names were switched. The upcoming presentation at 2:30 will be given by Dr. Mary Robinson, not Dr. Chuck Stein.（議程表有誤，兩位講者的姓名被對調。接下來的兩點半的場次將由 Mary Robinson 博士發表，而非 Chuck Stein 博士。），對照議程表後，可知兩點半與四點半的場次的講者需對調。最後又說 now let's welcome the speaker of this session, Dr. Mary Robinson, to the stage.（現在讓我們歡迎本場次的講者 Mary Robinson 博士上台。）根據更正後的議程表可得知 Mary Robinson 博士的發表地點為 South Hall，故正確答案為 B。

Time	Paper Presentation	
	Speaker(s)	Location
1:10	Daniel Brown	Main Auditorium
2:30	~~Chuck Stein~~ Mary Robinson	South Hall
3:30	Julia Yeh	~~East Hall~~ Central Hall
4:30	~~Mary Robinson~~ Chuck Stein	Central Hall

關鍵字詞 switch 調換

According to the announcement, when will Dr. Chuck Stein's session begin?

根據宣布事項，Chuck Stein 博士的場次何時開始？

A.　At 1:10.

B.　At 2:30.

C.　At 3:30.

D.　At 4:30.

A.　1:10

B.　2:30

C.　3:30

D.　4:30

正解　Ⓓ

本題同樣也需要整合宣布事項與議程表的多項訊息，才能掌握關鍵資訊。根據上題更正的議程表我們可得知 Chuck Stein 博士的場次應為 4:30。

🔍 關鍵字詞

接著我們來複習本部份的重點詞彙

gear 名 裝備（第 26 題）

例句 • Besides your camping gear, bring along at least three liters of water since there will be none available until we reach the campground.
除了要帶露營裝備，也要帶至少三公升的水，因為直到我們抵達營地才會有水。

• To stay overnight in a mountain, climbers need to be equipped with gear like cooking utensils and tents.
在山上過夜，登山者需要像是炊具和帳篷的裝備。

workout 名 鍛鍊（第 27 題）

例句 • The hike will take us about eight hours, so be prepared for a real workout.
這趟健行將會長達八小時，所以大家要準備好面對真正的鍛鍊。

• Regular workouts help one stay healthy and fit.
規律健身有助維持健康的體態。

intend 動 打算（第 28 題）

例句 • They'll be moving back to Germany soon, and they intend to sell their car.
他們很快會搬回德國，所以打算把車賣掉。

• Although the director is at the age of 65, she does not intend to retire this year.
雖然主任屆齡六十五歲，但她今年不打算退休。

延伸學習 intend to V; intend V-ing 打算做某事

condition 名 狀況（第 29 題）

例句
- They bought their car seven years ago but it's still in excellent condition.
  他們七年前買的車，但現在車況還很好。

- Hospital cleaning protocols are established to ensure the sanitary condition of all areas.
  醫院清潔守則是為了確保所有區域的衛生狀態。

延伸學習　in excellent condition 處於極佳狀況
　　　　　in critical condition 處於危急情況

tournament 名 錦標賽（第 30 題）

例句
- During the Wimbledon tournament, a handler would fly a hawk around the courts several times before matches began.
  在溫布頓網球錦標賽期間，每局之前馴鷹師會在球場周邊放飛老鷹數次。

- Tickets to the Wimbledon tennis tournament always sell out quickly because people want to watch the games in the flesh.
  溫布頓網球錦標賽的門票總是銷售迅速，因為很多人希望現場觀賽。

droppings 名 (動物的) 排泄物（第 30 題）

例句
- While looking for food, the pigeons would fly around the courts and dirty them with their droppings.
  鴿子一邊找尋食物、一邊飛遍球場，同時鴿子排泄物也會弄髒球場。

- The droppings scattered across the trail indicated that some sheep had recently passed by.
  從步道上遍灑的糞便看來，一些羊才剛經過。

hygiene 名 衛生（第 30 題）

例句
- Hygiene is the first priority in managing school cafeterias.
  管理學校餐廳的優先考量是衛生。

bird of prey 名 猛禽（第 31 題）

例句
- The eagle is a bird of prey, hunting to survive.
  老鷹是一種猛禽，靠捕獵維生。

tulip 名 鬱金香（第 32 題）

例句
- If you have a garden, then you may want to consider tulips and other blooming plants that grow from bulbs.
  如果你有一座花園，你可能會考慮種鬱金香和其他球莖花卉。

- The national flower of the Netherlands is the tulip though it originated from Turkey.
  荷蘭的國花是鬱金香，雖然它實際上源自土耳其。

bulb 名 球莖（第 32 題）

例句
- Generally speaking, the ideal time to plant bulbs is in the fall.
  一般而言，種植球莖的理想時間是秋天。

- If you plant these bulbs here, the flowers will look beautiful when they bloom in the spring.
  如果你在這種植這些球莖，春天時花會開得漂亮。

guidance 名 指引、指導（第 32 題）

例句
- This talk mainly provides guidance on planting and purchasing bulbs.
  此段談話主要提供種植與購買球莖的指引。

- With the advisor's guidance, the student's research paper was accepted by a prestigious journal.
  遵循指導教授的建議，這個學生的研究論文被一家知名期刊選用。

measurement 名 測量（第 33 題）

例句
- Accurate measurements can help you decide how many bulbs you should buy since each bulb type requires a different amount of space to thrive.
  準確的測量可幫助你決定要購買多少球莖，因為每種球莖生長所需的空間不同。

- The measurement of air pollution relies on various devices and records.
  空氣汙染的測量需仰賴數種儀器和紀錄。

thrive 動 茁壯（第 33 題）

例句
- My neighbor's wedding business has thrived for more than two decades, mainly because their dresses are beautiful.
  我鄰居的婚禮事業蓬勃發展超過二十年，主要因為他們的禮服很美。

bruise 名 碰傷、瘀傷（第 34 題）

例句
- Pick those bulbs that are free of bruises and soft spots.
  挑選無碰傷與壓起來不會軟軟的球莖。

- The child got a bruise on his leg because he slipped on the floor this morning.
  這個小孩腿上有瘀傷，因為早上他在地板滑倒。

tenant 名 房客（第 35 題）

例句
- The tenant's key got stuck in the lock, so we had a locksmith install a new lock.
  房客的鑰匙卡在鎖裡，所以我們請了鎖匠來安裝一副新鎖。

- The owner of the apartment called the tenant to ask if she would continue renting the room.
  公寓房東致電房客，詢問她是否要繼續租房。

overdue 形 過期（第 36 題）

例句
- Matthew will visit Mr. Smith in the afternoon and collect the overdue payment.
  Matthew 下午會拜訪 Smith 先生，收取遲繳的費用。

- The overdue membership can be renewed via online application, and then the music streaming services will resume.
  透過線上申請可以更新過期的會員資格，重啟音樂串流服務。

smoke alarm 名 煙霧偵測器（第 37 題）

例句
- I examined the smoke alarm in 9-A. There was nothing seriously wrong.
  我檢查了 9-A 的煙霧偵測器，並沒有嚴重問題。

- The old man, who was smoking in the bathroom, accidentally set off the smoke alarm.
  這位老人在廁所吸菸，不小心觸發了煙霧偵測器。

alteration 名 變更（第 38 題）

例句
- There have been several alterations to today's schedule.
  今日的議程有幾項變動。

- The tailor made some alterations to the gown so that it would fit the model.
  這位裁縫師做了一些修改，讓模特兒禮服合身。

switch 動 調換（第 39 題）

例句
- There was an error in the program. Two speakers' names were switched.
  議程裡有一個錯誤，兩位講者的名字調換了。

- The meeting was switched from Tuesday to Thursday due to the cancellation of my flight.
  因為我的航班取消了，所以會議從星期二改到星期四。

1. 認識多元的談話種類

中高級的談話類型多元，例如電台廣告（radio commercial）、新聞報導（news report）、演講 / 授課（lecture）、公共場所廣播（public announcement）或是人物敘述（narrative）等。平日應多積極主動接觸這些不同的談話方式、常用詞彙、內容發展的邏輯，熟悉不同類型的談話，才能在應試時發揮實力。

2. 系統化擴充生活中常用詞彙

聽力理解與字彙量息息相關。字彙累積到一定程度後，可以用同義字詞為基礎持續擴充單字量，例如動詞 use（使用）可以用 employ、utilize 來表達；動詞 get（獲得）則可以用 acquire 或 obtain 表達，學習更精準的字彙，才能在符號運用與溝通表達上更加精確、靈活、有效。

3. 練習「跟讀」技巧

談話題型的聽力題目需要藉由語音得知語意。有時候閱讀一個字，可以認出意思，但若改為聽同一個字，卻不一定知道意思。造成這樣的問題有可能是因為接觸的頻率不足以讓這個字內化成知識的一部份，另一個原因是因為對於發音掌握度不夠。前者可以透過廣泛閱讀得以進步，而後者則可以透過「跟讀」訓練，幫助掌握正確發音、加強聽力理解。「跟讀」一詞的英文是 shadowing，即是像影子跟著音檔的說話者複誦。實際上要怎麼練習呢？

(1) 找一個符合自己程度的影片或是音檔。一開始可找一至兩分鐘的影片或音檔，例如本書所附的音檔就很適合，隨著越來越進步，再增加長度。

(2) 多聽幾遍音檔，熟悉並理解內容。音檔或影片最好找有附錄音稿或字幕的，對照錄音稿查詢不認識的單字，並完整理解內容。

(3) 在不看錄音稿與字幕的情況下，同步複誦聽到的句子，與說話者之間只有一至兩秒的落差。請跟上說話者的語速，並試著模仿他的發音、重音、語調以及在何處停頓等。同時將自己的練習錄下。

(4) 比較自己的說話方式與音檔說話者的不同之處，再做調整，反覆練習。長久練習後不但可加強聽力，亦可增進口說能力。

4. 練習組織筆記

連續言談的重點可能不只有一個，所以筆記技巧格外重要，平時可以上網觀看英文演說影片、在學校選修英文授課的課程或是參加全程英文的講座，都是很適合實際演練英文筆記技巧的資源。剛開始選擇英文影片時，可以長度、主題作為選擇影片的基準，並調整影片的播放速度，循序漸進。最後，主動檢討筆記並規劃改進策略，可有效持續精進聽解與溝通表達的能力。

閱讀測驗

第一部份

詞彙

閱讀測驗 第一部份 詞彙

這部份共 10 題，每題均含有一個空格，根據題意選一個最適合的字或詞作答。

本部份評量的學習表現包括：

✓ 能辨識廣泛的詞彙（請參考全民英檢中高級字表）
✓ 能掌握詞彙在句子中的用法

考前提醒

這部份評量考生是否能在多元的情境中適切運用習得的詞彙和用語。這些詞彙皆是日常生活、學校或是工作情境中常用詞彙。題目會提供一個完整的情境，須根據該情境與上下文線索選擇最適合的詞彙。

平日加強詞彙時，應具備積極探究的態度，主動透過大量閱讀來熟悉詞彙如何實際運用在句子裡，並善用英英字典、搭配詞典等工具書強化自主學習，而非只是記下中文翻譯。

作答時

1. 留意搭配詞與關鍵詞彙

   如果遇到題目裡不知道意思的字詞不須緊張，答題線索常常不只一個，可試著根據句子裡其他與該情境相關的字詞或是搭配字詞（例如第 1 題），從選項中選出最適合的答案。

2. 運用語法結構的知識推測語意

   中高級的題目情境多元、句構也較豐富，包括倒裝句、假設語氣、分詞構句等。作答時可分析句構，找出句子的主詞、動詞與受詞。掌握句子結構可以幫助釐清語意關係，加速理解題意（例如第 9 題）。

3. 多留意連接詞，理解子句間的關係

   由於中高級題目的句子有時較長，會包含多個子句，子句間常以連接詞連接，多留意句子所使用的連接詞，才能正確掌握子句間的關係，幫助理解完整句意（例如第 2 題）。

4. 看完整句後再作答：務必看完整個句子，掌握全部的資訊後，再作答。這麼做才不會漏掉答題線索。

運用這些小撇步，可以從容釐清解題關鍵，累積答題經驗！

This valley offers some prime spots for viewing the awesome _____ of the monarch butterfly migration.

A. trophy

B. spectacle

C. outrage

D. vibration

山谷裡有些地點正適合觀賞帝王斑蝶遷徙的壯觀景色。

A. 戰利品

B. 奇觀

C. 駭人聽聞的行為

D. 震動

正解 B

本題為自然生態情境，必須根據句子描述的內容和搭配詞用法找出最適合此句的名詞。

句子提到可在山谷觀賞帝王斑蝶遷徙，選項中與情境相關，且可與 awesome（令人驚嘆的）搭配的字彙為 spectacle，因此正確答案為 B。

關鍵字詞 spectacle 奇觀 migration 遷徙

第 2 題

Linda gave away her leather sofa because it _____ too much space in her apartment.

A. took up

B. filled out

C. put away

D. stood for

Linda 將她的皮沙發送人，因為在她的公寓裡太佔地方了。

A. 佔據（空間、時間）

B. 填寫

C. 歸位

D. 代表

正解 Ⓐ

本題為一般生活情境。留意本句中所使用的連接詞 because，掌握語意的因果關係，就可以找出最適合此句的動詞片語。

句子說明將沙發送人的原因，由空格後的 too much space 可推知 Linda 認為沙發太佔位置了。根據選項的語意，得知正確答案為 A。有些人會選 B：filled out，意思為「填寫資料」，句子的主詞須為人，但本題 because 子句的主詞為沙發（it），語意、用法均不符，因此非正確答案。

關 鍵 字 詞　give away 贈送、捐贈　take up 佔據（空間、時間）

The Liberal Party enjoyed wide public support and was predicted to win _____ victory in the election.

A. an underlying

B. a simultaneous

C. a renowned

D. an overwhelming

自由黨廣受民眾支持，預期本次選舉會大獲全勝。

A. 潛在的

B. 同時的

C. 有名的

D. 壓倒性的

正解 D

本題取材自政治議題，必須根據題目描述的內容找出最適合此句的形容詞。

本句提到自由黨很受歡迎，預期會在選舉獲勝，選項中與情境最相關的字彙為 overwhelming，表示將獲得壓倒性勝利（overwhelming victory）。

關鍵字詞 overwhelming 壓倒性的

第 4 題

As part of routine maintenance, technicians _____ inspect every computer on the department's network.

技術人員進行的例行維修包括定期檢查部門網路的每台電腦。

A. conversely

B. exclusively

C. periodically

D. tentatively

A. 相反地

B. 專有地

C. 定期地

D. 躊躇地

正解 Ⓒ

本題取材自工作情境。必須根據題目描述的情境和搭配詞用法，找出最適合此句的副詞。

題目選項均為副詞，而該副詞修飾的動詞是 inspect（檢查），四個選項中較適合修飾此動詞的副詞僅有 B 跟 C。句子前半部告訴我們，這個檢查是例行維修的一部份（As part of routine maintenance），因此可推知選項 C：periodically（定期地），較符合情境，因此正確答案為 C。

關鍵字詞　maintenance 維修　periodically 定期地

Although not as common as fifty years ago, arranged marriages are still _____ in parts of China.

A. redundant

B. reckless

C. prevalent

D. perpetual

在中國,媒妁之言的婚姻雖然不如五十年前常見,但在部份地區仍很普遍。

A. 多餘的

B. 魯莽的

C. 普遍的

D. 永久的

正解 C

本題取材自中國的文化習俗。本題的答題關鍵在於句中使用的連接詞 although(雖然)和副詞 still(仍然),理解兩個子句的對立關係,便可找出最適合此句的形容詞。

前半句說媒妁之言的婚姻已較少見,由連接詞 although 和副詞 still 可推知下半句描述的情況與上半句不同。根據選項的語意,得知正確答案為 C。有些人會選 A,但 redundant 的負面語意與情境不符。

關鍵字詞 prevalent 普遍的

第 6 題

The mayor's comments were supposed to be _____, but the media quoted them in many news reports.

A. off the record

B. out of order

C. on the rise

D. out of the blue

市長的言論本應是非公開的，但卻被媒體在許多報導中引用。

A. 不公開的

B. 故障的

C. 在上升

D. 出乎意料

正解 Ⓐ

本題取材自政治議題，需要根據兩個子句的對立關係找出最適合的介係詞片語。

後半句說媒體在諸多報導中引用市長的言論（them），由連接詞 but 可知前後兩個子句的語意有對立關係。根據選項的語意，得知正確答案為 A，表示言論本來應是非公開的。

關鍵字詞 off the record 不公開的

The volcano has _____ more than thirty times in recorded history. Once it even buried a town in several feet of ash.

A. revolted

B. faltered

C. crumbled

D. erupted

根據歷史紀錄，這座火山已噴發 30 餘次，其中一次火山灰堆積好幾英尺，掩埋了一整座城鎮。

A. 反叛

B. 動搖

C. 崩潰

D. 爆發

正解 D

本題為自然生態情境，必須綜合兩句話的內容和搭配詞用法找出最適合此句的動詞。

本題描述火山的活動，第二句說火山灰曾掩埋一座城鎮，可推測本題談論的是火山爆發。選項中與情境相關，且可與 volcano（火山）搭配的字彙為 erupted，因此正確答案為 D。其他選項不論語意或是搭配用法皆與本題不合。

關鍵字詞 erupt 爆發的

第 8 題

A non-smoker who breathes second-hand smoke is exposed to _____ 3,700 chemicals.

A. frankly

B. roughly

C. solely

D. briefly

不吸菸者吸入二手菸時，會接觸到大約 3,700 種化學物質。

A. 坦白地

B. 大約

C. 唯一

D. 短暫地

正解　B

本題為健康醫藥情境，必須根據題目描述的內容和搭配詞用法找出最適合此句的副詞。

空格後為 **3,700 chemicals**（3,700 種化學物質），選項中能修飾數量的為 **roughly**，且語意和句子情境相符，因此正確答案為 **B**。

關鍵字詞　roughly 大約

The United Nations passed a resolution _____ the country for conducting a nuclear test last week.

A. condemning

B. ascertaining

C. irritating

D. nominating

聯合國通過決議，譴責該國於上週進行核試。

A. 譴責

B. 確認

C. 使惱怒

D. 提名

正解 A

本題取材自政治議題，必須根據題目描述的因果關係並利用語法知識找出最適合的動詞。掌握本句的句子結構亦有助理解語意。首先可將本句的內容分析如下：

行動	The United Nations passed a resolution _____ the country （聯合國通過決議 _____ 該國）
原因	for conducting a nuclear test last week （因〔該國〕於上週進行核試。）

根據選項的語意，得知選項 A 最適合本句情境，表示因為某國家進行核試而決定加以譴責。irritate 語意與聯合國決議無關；ascertain 後面通常接 that 子句，表示「確認某件事情」；nominate 後面接「受詞＋for/as＋名詞」，表示「提名某人擔任某職務」，用法不符。

另外，分析本句的句構可得知，本句省略關係代名詞，將關係子句中的動詞改為現在分詞的句型，因此原句為 The United Nations passed a resolution <u>which condemned</u> the country for conducting a nuclear test last week. 了解這個句構後可幫助正確理解此句語意。

關鍵字詞 condemn 譴責

第 10 題

Please make an appointment if you wish to discuss your investment options in _____ with one of our financial advisers.

A. need

B. effect

C. depth

D. all

如果您想與理財專員深入討論您的投資選擇，敬請預約諮詢。

A. 需要的（in need）

B. 實際上（in effect）

C. 深入地（in depth）

D. 總共（in all）

正解 Ⓒ

本題取材自工作情境，必須根據題目描述的內容和搭配詞用法找出最適合的片語。

空格前為 discuss your investment options（討論你的投資選擇），選項中可修飾 discuss 的片語為 in depth，且語意與情境相符，因此正確答案為 C。

關鍵字詞 in depth 深入地

接著我們來複習本部份的重點詞彙

spectacle 名 奇觀（第 1 題）

例句
- This valley offers some prime spots for viewing the awesome spectacle of the monarch butterfly migration.
  山谷裡有些地點正適合觀賞帝王斑蝶遷徙的壯觀景色。

- Every year, large numbers of tourists visit Mountain Ali to witness the amazing spectacle of the sun rising above clouds.
  每年大批遊客造訪阿里山，為了目睹日出雲海的奇觀。

migration 名 遷徙（第 1 題）

例句
- On the one hand, migration is a driving force of knowledge transfer, but on the other hand, it causes competition for resources.
  人口遷移一方面成為知識轉移的驅力，另一方面造就資源競爭。

give away 贈送、捐贈（第 2 題）

例句
- Linda gave away her leather sofa because it took up too much space in her apartment.
  Linda 將她的皮沙發送人，因為在她的公寓裡太佔地方了。

- We should sort the clothes into different categories before giving them away to charity.
  我們應該要先分類衣物，再捐贈至慈善機構。

take up 佔據（空間、時間）（第 2 題）

例句
- Sleep takes up most of a koala's time as much as twenty-two hours per day.
  睡眠佔據無尾熊大多數的時間，一天最多可多達 22 小時。

overwhelming 形 壓倒性的（第 3 題）

例句
- The Liberal Party enjoyed wide public support and was predicted to win an overwhelming victory in the election.
  自由黨廣受民眾支持，預期本次選舉會大獲全勝。

- Surprisingly, the newly established party won an overwhelming victory, obtaining 76% of the votes.
  令人驚訝地，新成立的政黨獲得壓倒性勝利，得到百分之七十六的選票。

maintenance 名 維修（第 4 題）

例句
- As part of routine maintenance, technicians periodically inspect every computer on the department's network.
  技術人員進行的例行維修包括定期檢查部門網路的每台電腦。

- The elevator is under maintenance, so we have no choice but to climb the stairs to our office on the ninth floor.
  電梯正在維修中，所以我們只能爬樓梯到九樓辦公室。

periodically 副 定期地（第 4 題）

例句
- Textbooks should be updated periodically so that their content can reflect changes in society.
  教科書應定期修訂，以期內容能夠與時俱進。

prevalent 形 普遍的（第 5 題）

例句
- Although not as common as fifty years ago, arranged marriages are still prevalent in parts of China.
  在中國，媒妁之言的婚姻雖然不如五十年前常見，但在部份地區仍很普遍。

- While the use of headphones with mobile devices has long been common, wireless earphones have only recently become prevalent.
  耳罩式耳機連結手機的使用已經相當常見，而無線耳塞式耳機則是最近才普遍。

off the record 不公開的（第 6 題）

例句 • The mayor's comments were supposed to be off the record, but the media quoted them in many news reports.
市長的言論本應是非公開的，但卻被媒體在許多報導中引用。

• The president asked for his comments to be kept off the record until the emergency was over.
直到緊急事件解除之前，總統要求暫不公開他的評論。

erupt 動 爆發（第 7 題）

例句 • The volcano has erupted more than thirty times in recorded history. Once it even buried a town in several feet of ash.
根據歷史紀錄，這座火山已噴發 30 餘次，其中一次火山灰堆積好幾英尺，掩埋了一整座城鎮。

• The volcano may erupt so residents nearby were warned to leave the area as soon as possible.
火山可能會爆發，所以附近居民被警告儘速離開該區域。

roughly 副 大約（第 8 題）

例句 • A non-smoker who breathes second-hand smoke is exposed to roughly 3,700 chemicals.
不吸菸者吸入二手菸時，會接觸到大約 3,700 種化學物質。

• The teacher roughly sketched an outline of the mug before demonstrating how to control light and darkness using a pencil.
老師大略勾勒出馬克杯的輪廓，接著示範如何用鉛筆表現明暗。

condemn 動 譴責（第 9 題）

例句 • The United Nations passed a resolution condemning the country for conducting a nuclear test last week.
聯合國通過決議，譴責該國於上週進行核試。

• The society condemned the company for dumping chemical wastes into the river.
這家公司受到社會譴責，因為他們傾倒化學廢料進河流。

延伸學習 condemn someone for V-ing 譴責某人做了…

in depth 深入地（第 10 題）

例句
- Please make an appointment if you wish to discuss your investment options in depth with one of our financial advisers.
  如果您想與理財專員深入討論您的投資選擇，敬請預約諮詢。

- If you want to explore this country in depth, I would suggest you get to know some locals and their lifestyles.
  如果你想要深入探索這個國家，我建議你認識當地人，並體驗他們的生活方式。

Note

💡 學習策略

1. 系統性觀察字根、字首、字尾，提升符號運用與溝通表達的能力

有些英文字彙有相同的字根，表示它們都是從同一個概念延伸出的字彙，可以利用英文的這個特色，了解一些相近的詞彙，例如 <u>differ</u>（與⋯不同）、<u>different</u>（不同的）、<u>differentiate</u>（分辨、區別）、<u>differential</u>（差別的）、in<u>differ</u>ent（不感興趣的）。此外，也能利用字首或字尾辨別語意或詞性，例如字首 "de" 通常表示「反轉、去除」之意，像是 <u>detach</u>（分開）、<u>decompose</u>（分解）、<u>decode</u>（解碼）、<u>degenerate</u>（退化）、<u>decrease</u>（減少）；字尾 "ate" 則含有「行動」之意，因此以 ate 結尾的字大部份都是動詞，像是 accumul<u>ate</u>（累積）、circul<u>ate</u>（循環）、demonstr<u>ate</u>（示範）、evacu<u>ate</u>（撤離）、facilit<u>ate</u>（促進）等。透過字根、字首、字尾，不論是學習新單字或是理解題目時，都能夠提供相當的助力。

2. 積極探索相關主題和議題，擴充詞彙量

例如，當讀到一篇主題為生物燃料（biofuel）的文章時，可利用關鍵字搜尋相關主題的文章，主動記下相關的英文詞彙怎麼說，像是 renewable energy（再生能源）、carbon dioxide（二氧化碳）、emission（排放）、動詞則是 emit（排放）等。像這樣系統化地累積同一主題的字彙，下次閱讀相關主題的文章或句子時便能較快理解文意。

3. **主動運用英英字典有效提升個人英語文知能，更精準地學習單字**

有些英文字彙的中文翻譯相近，造成學習者誤解兩個字互為同義字，實際上卻是很不一樣的兩個字。例如 doubt 和 suspect 的中文常常翻譯為「懷疑」，但若查閱英英字典，就會發現兩者的語意不同。doubt 指的是對於某事物感到不確定，而 suspect 則是認為或相信某事物為真或為可能的，舉例來說，I doubt that he stole my money. 表示「我不認為他偷了我的錢。」而 I suspect that he stole my money. 則表示「我認為他偷了我的錢。」兩者語意其實是相反的。如果僅翻閱英漢字典，就會錯失一些重要的語意細節。

4. **了解詞彙不同的語意與用法，在多元情境中展現適切溝通表達的能力**

一個單字或是片語常常不只有一個意思，學習時可以參考字典中的各個例句或是留意詞彙在文章中使用的情境與方式，才能掌握正確的語意與用法。例如，take up 這個片語在不同的上下文中有不一樣的意思，在本部份第 2 題中，The sofa took up too much space in her apartment.，它表示「佔據」，但在 When she left home, she took up cooking. 這個句子中，take up 則是「開始做某事」之意，若沒有參照例句或文章，便不容易掌握正確語意與用法。

閱讀測驗
第二部份

段落填空

閱讀測驗 第二部份 段落填空

這部份有兩個段落,每個段落中有數個空格,須根據文意、句構、上下文邏輯從選項中選出最適合題意的字或詞,以還原題意。

本部份評量的學習表現包括:

- ✓ 能辨識廣泛的詞彙(請參考全民英檢中高級字表)
- ✓ 能掌握詞彙和語法規則的用法
- ✓ 能根據上下文語境釐清兩個訊息間的關係
- ✓ 能利用字詞結構、上下文意句型及篇章組織推測字義或句子內容

考前提醒

這部份評量重點為常用詞彙與語法結構。考生除了需能將習得的詞彙和語法結構運用於新情境,還需釐清文章的脈絡與前後句子邏輯的關係,才能選出最符合篇章銜接與連貫的選項。

作答時，你可以

1. 分析句構理解語意，建立前後句或子句間的邏輯關係

遇到較長的句子不要緊張，找出句子的主詞、動詞與受詞，透過句構掌握句意（例如第16、20 題），更能快速察覺缺少的語意。看到長句也可以快速理解。

2. 確實掌握代名詞的用法

代名詞是為了避免反覆提及前文中出現的人或物而使用，可以避免累贅，讓行文更俐落。確實了解代名詞所代替的詞彙，可以幫助釐清上下文的語意邏輯（例如第11 題）。

3. 掌握字詞的連貫性

段落中通常會使用不同的字、詞重複闡述意見或概念，加強文章的連貫性。掌握此關鍵可以提高閱讀的速度並加強理解，例如 The coffee shop added the delivery service ten months ago.（十個月前這家咖啡廳增加外送服務）This change has led to its growing popularity among nearby office workers.（這項改變愈來愈受到附近上班族的歡迎），This change 指的是咖啡廳增加外送服務。在以下兩個題組中都可以看到這個寫作機制（第 15 題後的 This business、第 19、20 題的 this menace、vulnerable shipping lanes 和 this crime）。藉由理解這樣的連貫性特點，可以更精準找出上下文語意關係。

透過以上技巧，可以減少閱讀理解過程中可能遇到的困難，順利推敲正解！

Hand-made glass beads have played an important role in the culture of the Paiwan, one of Taiwan's native aboriginal tribes. Traditionally, these ornaments were the property of upper-class members of the Paiwan tribe, （11） them on ceremonial occasions. （12） their heritage, each generation of tribal leaders passed their beads down to their children. In the twentieth century, though, this particular aspect of Paiwan culture declined. Many of the tribe's precious bead collections were broken up, （13） individual beads were sold to buyers in cities. In the 1980s, members of the tribe took it upon themselves to （14） the Paiwan bead culture and the bead-making art. Through trial and error, they developed their own techniques for making traditional as well as modern bead designs. Their creations were so successful with tourists that a bead-making industry was established. （15） This business also secures a key part of Paiwan culture for the future.

本段落為一篇說明文，主題是排灣族的琉璃珠工藝。文章說明在古代，琉璃珠是貴族階級的傳家之寶，供參加祭典時配戴，但這個習俗已經沒落，許多琉璃珠被變賣。1980 年代，排灣族人決心復興琉璃珠文化，成功發展琉璃珠工藝，廣受觀光客歡迎。

Note

第 11 題

A.　and wore	A.　且配戴（連接詞加過去式）
B.　who wore	B.　配戴（關係代名詞加過去式）
C.　have worn	C.　已經配戴（現在完成式）
D.　were wearing	D.　在配戴（過去進行式）

正解　B

本題評量關係代名詞 who 的用法。作答時，需理解空格前後子句的邏輯關係和空格後的代名詞 them 所指稱的對象。

空格所在句子分析如下：

主要子句	these ornaments were the property of upper-class members of the Paiwan tribe（這些飾品為排灣族貴族所有）
從屬子句	_____ them on ceremonial occasions（於祭典 __ 它們）

根據選項共同的詞彙 wear，可知空格後的代名詞 them 指的正是前一個子句中的 these ornaments。選項 B 填入後表示貴族於祭典配戴這些飾品，用 who 代表空格前的 upper-class members of the Paiwan tribe，語意、用法皆相符，因此為正確答案。

若填入 and wore，後半句的主詞會與主要子句的主詞相同，皆為 ornaments，語意則為「這些飾品在典禮配戴飾品」，不合邏輯；若填入 have worn 或 were wearing，則兩個子句間欠缺連接詞，語法不正確。

關鍵字詞　ornament 裝飾品

A. Regardless of preserving	A. 不管保存
B. Being preserved	B. 被保存
C. In order to preserve	C. 為了保存
D. By means of preserving	D. 藉由保存

正解 Ⓒ

本題評量不定詞片語的語意和用法。先掌握主要子句和片語間的邏輯關係，理解語意關聯後，對照選項中句型的用法，便能推測最適合的語意與結構。

根據選項共同的詞彙 preserve（保存）和空格所在句子的語意，推測本句欲表達的內容為：

目的	_____ their heritage（_____ 他們的文化遺產）
手段	each generation of tribal leaders passed their beads down to their children.（一代代的部落領袖將珠子傳給子孫）

根據句子間的邏輯關係，得知空格應填入不定詞片語 In order to preserve，表達「為了要保存文化遺產」，如此一來語意邏輯通順且語法結構正確。

regardless of 通常接名詞（例如：age、consequence、risk）而非動名詞，且語意「不論」也不適切；being preserved（被保存）為被動式，後面不會接名詞當受詞，因此選項 A、B 用法不符。by means of 表示「藉由」，通常用來說明手段、方法，與本句邏輯關係相反。

關鍵字詞 heritage（文化）遺產 pass...down 世代相傳

第 13 題

A. yet	A. 但是
B. as	B. 隨著
C. whether	C. 是否
D. only if	D. 只當

正解 Ⓑ

本題評量連接詞的語意。掌握兩個子句間的邏輯關係，對照各選項語意，選出最適切的連接詞。

本句內容分析如下：

結果／發生在後	Many of the tribe's precious bead collections were broken up（許多收藏於部落的珍貴琉璃珠被拆散）
原因／發生在前	individual beads were sold to buyers in cities（個別的珠子被市區的買家蒐購）

這兩個子句的語意有「時間先後／因果」的關聯性，因此正確答案為 B（隨著個別的珠子被市區的買家蒐購，許多收藏於部落的珍貴琉璃珠被拆散）。其他選項的語意均不符。

關鍵字詞 break up 拆散

A.	subscribe	A.	訂購、贊成
B.	provoke	B.	激怒
C.	testify	C.	作證
D.	revive	D.	使復甦

正解 D

本題評量動詞的語意和用法，作答時需了解上下文語意並參考搭配詞用法。

關鍵句型為 S take it upon oneself to do something，意思為「某人主動承擔責任去做某事」，空格句的語意為「排灣族人主動 ＿＿＿＿ 琉璃珠工藝」。

解題線索在整合上下文語意。前文提到 this particular aspect of Paiwan culture declined（琉璃珠逐漸式微），對照問題句後一句的語意 Through trial and error, they developed their own techniques for making traditional as well as modern bead designs.（透過反覆嘗試，他們研發出製作傳統與現代風格琉璃珠的生產技術）。根據兩個句子之間呈現的對比，得知空格應填入 revive，表示族人開始復興這項傳統文化。選項 B、C 語意與情境不符。subscribe 雖然語意勉強符合上下文邏輯，但須接上 to + 名詞，用法不符。

關 鍵 字 詞　revive 使復甦　take it upon oneself to 自告奮勇（做）

第 15 題　　New!

A. Today it provides employment for trained aboriginal artists in Paiwan villages.

B. Elders usually wear single strings of white beads made of pearl or ivory around their neck.

C. To improve revenue, the factory has started giving tours and opened a craft shop.

D. The traditional ones bear ancient designs that look aesthetically pleasing and powerful.

A. 現今它為排灣部落裡受過訓練的原鄉藝術家帶來工作機會。

B. 長者通常脖子上掛著白色珍珠或象牙製成的單串項鍊。

C. 為了增加營收，工廠開始提供導覽並開設了手作坊。

D. 傳統的樣式採用美感和張力十足的古老設計。

正解　Ⓐ

本題的重點在於統整歸納多個句子的資訊，作答時須從空格前、後的句子掌握字詞的連貫性，並判斷最符合文章邏輯發展的選項。

空格前後內容分析如下：

前一句介紹的主題	a bead-making industry was established（發展了琉璃珠製造產業）
空格句	正解
後一句的內容：**另一項**影響	This business **also** secures a key part of Paiwan culture for the future.（**並且**，這個產業為後世保存排灣族文化的重要一環。）

This business 指的便是前一句的 bead-making industry。由於空格句後一句使用 "also" 引出琉璃珠產業的另一影響，因此可推論空格句的內容應該是琉璃珠產業的第一個影響。選項中提到本產業影響的只有 A：帶來工作機會，因此為正確答案。

關 鍵 字 詞　aboriginal 原住民的

接著我們來複習本部份的重點詞彙

ornament **名** 裝飾品（第 11 題）

例句
- Traditionally, these ornaments were the property of upper-class members of the Paiwan tribe, who wore them on ceremonial occasions.
  傳統上，這些裝飾品為排灣族貴族階級所有，他們會在祭典中佩戴這些裝飾品。

- In early December, my family would decorate our Christmas tree with ornaments, flowers, and ribbons.
  12 月初，我的家人會用裝飾品、花和蝴蝶結布置聖誕樹。

heritage **名** （文化）遺產（第 12 題）

例句
- In order to preserve their heritage, each generation of tribal leaders passed their beads down to their children.
  為了要保存他們的文化遺產，一代代的部落領袖將珠子傳給子孫。

- The world heritage site has been described as "our legacy from the past," and its preservation and protection rely on the efforts of all human beings.
  這個世界文化遺產景點被形容為「來自過往的傳承」，同時它的保存和保護仰賴全人類的努力。

pass down 世代相傳（第 12 題）

例句
- Storytelling is an effective method of passing down cultures and customs from one generation to the next.
  說故事是代代傳承文化和傳統的有效方式。

break up 拆散（第 13 題）

例句
- Many of the tribe's precious bead collections were broken up, as individual beads were sold to buyers in cities.
  隨著個別的珠子被市區的買家蒐購，許多收藏於部落的珍貴琉璃珠被拆散。

- The child broke up the jigsaw pieces, and one of them was missing.
  這個小孩打散了拼圖，遺失其中一塊。

revive 動 使復甦（第 14 題）

例句
- In the 1980s, members of the tribe took it upon themselves to revive the Paiwan bead culture and the bead-making art.
  在 1980 年代，排灣族人主動開始復興琉璃珠文化與工藝。

- Walking in nature revives my soul, so I love taking vacations in the mountains.
  大自然漫步可復甦心靈，因此我喜歡到山裡度假。

take it upon oneself to 自告奮勇（做）（第 14 題）

例句
- The voluntary group takes it upon itself to clean up the beach after national holidays.
  在國定假期之後，這個志工團體自發清理海灘。

aboriginal 形 原住民的（第 15 題）

例句
- Today it provides employment for trained aboriginal artists in Paiwan villages.
  今天它為排灣部落裡受過訓練的原鄉藝術家帶來工作機會。

- Tales from aboriginal history have been adapted into teaching materials so that students can learn more about the past of this land.
  原住民歷史故事被編製成教材，讓學生可以更加了解關於這塊土地的過去。

Piracy has become a critical danger to fishing boats and cargo ships in the waters off the coast of Somalia. Part of the problem is （16） for two decades this African country has lacked a well-organized central government. As a result, many Somalis who are struggling （17） resort to robbing ships. Rather than （18）, Somali gunmen traveling in speed boats have been seizing ships with the intent of obtaining ransoms for the release of hostages. With the aim of countering this menace, the world's major naval powers have sent warships to （19） the vulnerable shipping lanes. Experts caution that attempts to combat piracy must not be restricted to the high seas. Since piracy （20） to poverty and weak governments on land, naval power alone is unlikely to eliminate this crime. Such a response must be combined with diplomatic and humanitarian measures.

本段落為一篇說明文，主題是索馬利亞海盜猖獗的原因和反制力量。文章描述索馬利亞政府失能，民不聊生，百姓改以劫持商船並勒索贖金為業。強權國家為此派出軍艦保護航道，但專家認為需要配合其他手段才能解決問題。

第 16 題

A. during which

B. by the time

C. why

D. that

A. 在那段期間

B. 到那時

C. 為何

D. （引導子句的連接詞）

正解 Ⓓ

本題評量名詞子句連接詞 that 的用法。透過分析句構，可以發現原句語意已相當完整，須整合語法知識判斷哪一個選項既符合文法結構又不影響語意邏輯。

本句的結構分析如下：

主詞	Part of the problem （部份的問題）
動詞	is （是／在於）
子句	for two decades this African country has lacked a well-organized central government （過去 20 年這個非洲國家缺乏一個組織完善的中央政府）

雖然句子稍長，但不難理解語意。從語法層面來看，動詞 is 後方應接名詞或形容詞做為主詞的補語。雖然選項中的 why 和 that 皆可引導子句，但如果接 why 會造成語意不符邏輯，使用 that 引導子句則不影響句意邏輯，所以 D 為正確答案。during which 是關係代名詞的結構，但本句缺少它可代替的名詞，而 by the time 是用來連接兩個子句，兩個用法皆不符合此句。

關鍵字詞　decade 十年　well-organized 組織良好的

A. being survived
B. by surviving
C. to survive
D. having to survive

A. 生存（被動語態）
B. 生存（介係詞加現在分詞）
C. 生存（不定詞）
D. 生存（現在分詞加不定詞）

正解 Ⓒ

本題評量動詞的型態。本句的關鍵句型為 S struggle to V，意思為「某人努力做某事」，想表示「我努力工作賺錢」可以說 I struggle to make a living、「他努力想通過考試」He struggles to pass the test。

空格句的語意為「許多索馬利亞人為了要生存轉而劫持商船。」，選項中只有 C 符合 struggle 一字的常見用法，因此為正確答案。

關鍵字詞 resort to 訴諸、採取

第 18 題　　New!

A.　carrying sophisticated weapons

B.　stealing cargo from vessels

C.　recruiting desperate youth

D.　launching attacks at midnight

A.　攜帶先進武器

B.　竊取船上的貨物

C.　吸收鋌而走險的年輕人

D.　於半夜發動攻擊

 正解 Ⓑ

本題作答時，需統整歸納多個句子的資訊，根據空格前後句子以及介係詞 rather than 語意與用法，判斷最符合文章邏輯發展的選項。

空格前後內容分析如下：

前一句	As a result, many Somalis who are struggling to survive resort to **robbing ships**.（因此，許多索馬利亞人為了要生存轉而搶劫商船。）
空格句	**Rather than** _____, Somali gunmen traveling in speed boats have been seizing ships with the intent of obtaining ransoms for the release of hostages.（索馬利亞歹徒並未 _____，而是持槍搭乘快艇，劫持商船，索求贖金作為釋放人質的代價。）

四個選項都是以動名詞開頭，代表本題要考語意。句首的 **Rather than** 的意思是「並未、沒有」。由此可知空格內字詞與主要子句的內容相對，此外空格的前一句提到搶劫商船，可推知空格內應該會談論到與一般認知的搶劫行為有關，因此選項 B 的「竊取貨物」語意與情境上皆符合，表示「這些海盜沒有竊取貨物，反而劫持商船，索求贖金」，因此 B 為正確答案。選項 A 與 D 雖然也與搶劫行為相關，但是與空格後的語意（脅持人質，索求贖金）並非是相對的，故不是最合適的答案。而選項 C 則是與語意及情境不符。

關鍵字詞　ransom 贖金

A. deport
B. avert
C. patrol
D. trigger

A. 驅逐出境
B. 避免
C. 巡邏
D. 觸發

正解 C

本題評量動詞的語意。理解本句「目的─手段」的邏輯關係，應不難選出答案。

本句前半部份提到 With the aim of countering this menace（為了對抗海盜的威脅），大國派出軍艦 ___ 易受攻擊的航道；此處的 this menace 即是前述的劫盜行為。空格後為 vulnerable shipping lanes（易受攻擊的航道），指的是容易遭受海盜攻擊的航行路線。這兩處都是為了加強連貫性而出現的修辭，理解它們所代表的事物，更容易掌握完整語意。

整合前後語意，可知空格內應填入 patrol，表示為了對抗海盜而派出軍艦「巡邏」航道。

關鍵字詞 menace 威脅 patrol 巡邏 vulnerable 易受攻擊的、脆弱的

第 20 題

A. is linked
B. to be linked
C. having linked
D. should have linked

A. 相關（被動式）
B. 相關（不定詞）
C. 相關（動名詞）
D. 相關（完成式）

正解 A

本題評量動詞的型態，需掌握句子的結構和詞彙用法以正確選答。

本句是由 Since 連接的兩個子句所組成。空格所在的子句結構分析如下：

連接詞	Since（因為）
主詞	piracy（海盜打劫行為）
動詞	（20）
副詞片語	to poverty and weak governments on land（與貧窮問題以及陸上無能的政府）

由此可知，空格內需填入主要動詞，選項中 A 和 D 含有主要動詞，為可能答案。而不定詞（to be linked）和動名詞（having linked）非主要動詞，用法不符。Link 意指「與…相關」的時候，應使用被動式，而 is linked 為被動式，因此 A 為正確答案。

逗號後的子句 naval power alone is unlikely to eliminate this crime.（單靠海軍勢力無法消滅這種犯罪行為）。This crime 指的正是前文提到的持槍搭乘快艇，劫持商船，索求贖金等行為，這個修辭方式除了能增加字詞豐富度，更可以提升文章連貫性。

關鍵字詞　be linked to 與…相關

關鍵字詞

接著我們來複習本部份的重點詞彙

decade 名 十年（第 16 題）

例句
- Part of the problem is that for two decades this African country has lacked a well-organized central government.
  部份的問題在於過去 20 年這個非洲國家缺乏一個組織完善的中央政府。

- Only a decade ago, few could have imagined that being a YouTuber could be a career.
  不過十年前，人們難以想像 YouTuber 可以是一項職業。

well-organized 形 組織良好的（第 16 題）

例句
- The essay on artificial intelligence was so well-organized that even non-professionals easily understand the details.
  這篇關於人工智慧的文章組織良好，所以即使是非專業領域的人也容易了解細節。

resort to 訴諸、採取（第 17 題）

例句
- Many Somalis who are struggling to survive resort to robbing ships.
  許多索馬利亞人為了要生存轉而劫持商船。

- Since the barbecue restaurant was not willing to improve its ventilation system, its neighbor decided to resort to the law and reported it to the authorities.
  因為這家燒烤店不願意改善排煙系統，鄰居決定訴諸法律、提出申訴。

ransom 名 贖金（第 18 題）

例句
- Rather than stealing cargo from vessels, Somali gunmen traveling in speed boats have been seizing ships with the intent of obtaining ransoms for the release of hostages.
  索馬利亞歹徒沒有竊取船上的貨物，而是持槍搭乘快艇，劫持商船，索求贖金作為釋放人質的代價。

- The police advised the wife of the kidnap victim not to hand over the ransom demanded by the gang.
  警方告知綁架受害者的太太不要交出幫派要求的贖金。

menace 名 威脅（第 19 題）

例句
- With the aim of countering this menace, the world's major naval powers have sent warships to patrol the vulnerable shipping lanes.
  為了對抗海盜的威脅，世界主要海軍軍力派出軍艦巡邏易受攻擊的航道。

- Due to ultraviolet radiation, frequent exposure to the sun can be a menace to the health of one's eyes and skin.
  由於紫外線輻射，時常在太陽下曝曬會危害眼睛和皮膚的健康。

patrol 動 巡邏（第 19 題）

例句
- The loyal German Shepard dog accompanied a policeman patrolling every night.
  這隻忠心的德國牧羊犬每晚陪同警員巡邏。

vulnerable 形 易受攻擊的、脆弱的（第 19 題）

例句
- Until the bug is fixed, websites will be vulnerable to attacks from hackers.
  漏洞被修補之前，網站容易遭駭客入侵。

be linked to 與⋯相關（第 20 題）

例句
- Since piracy is linked to poverty and weak governments on land, naval power alone is unlikely to eliminate this crime.
  因為海盜盛行與貧窮問題以及陸上無能的政府有關，單靠海軍勢力無法消滅這種犯罪行為。

- Although the disease was originally linked to the change of a gene, there is actually little research evidence to support this.
  原先這個疾病被認為與基因變異有關，但事實上並無足夠證據支持這項關聯。

1. 閱讀英文文章或接觸英文媒體時，多留意搭配詞（collocation）

有時候受到母語或是翻譯的影響，會無法正確辨認符合真實語用的搭配詞，例如 heavy 一字意思為「重的」，字詞搭配「大雨」可以用 heavy rain，「濃妝」則是 heavy makeup，單從中文的「大」和「濃」無法想到 heavy 一字，需要讀過或聽過才可能知道，而累積多一點搭配詞，不但是為了答題而已，也能夠讓自己與英語母語人士溝通時有更適切的遣詞用字，與真實語用情境更為貼近，展現良好的符號運用與溝通表達能力。

2. 除了詞彙之外，使用正確的文法也是展現良好溝通互動素養的一環

例如本部份第 17 題 struggle 後面常見的一種結構是不定詞（to V），如果要表達努力生存，誤寫為 struggle surviving 就錯了；或例如第 20 題的 since 作為介係詞與連接詞時，使用的句構也不同，當 since 是介係詞，後面應接上代表一個時間點的名詞或動名詞（例如：last week 或是 returning from school 等），但是當它作為連接詞時，就要特別留意 since 後面要加上有主詞及動詞的完整子句才是正確的（例如：I was 10 years old 或是 they got married 等）。沒有正確的文法知識，便無法正確地使用英文。

3. 依據語意分類學習連接詞、轉折詞，幫助釐清上下文邏輯關係

閱讀文章時，留意作者所使用的連接詞與轉折詞，分析辨別它在上下文的語意，再依照類別記下這些詞彙，例如「與時間相關」的詞彙有 while、meanwhile、as soon as 等；欲「進一步說明」時可用 in other words、to put it differently 等；說明結果則常見 as a result、for that reason 等。這麼做可以幫助你在閱讀時迅速掌握前後句子的關係，加速釐清文章的論述邏輯。

Note

閱讀測驗
第三部份

閱讀理解

這部份共 20 題，包含數篇文章及圖表，每篇文章或圖表會搭配 2-6 個相關的問題。須先理解文章與圖表的內容，再根據問題，選出最適合者作答。

本部份評量的學習表現包括：

✓ 能閱讀不同體裁、主題的文章
✓ 能了解文章、書信的內容及文本結構
✓ 能熟悉各種閱讀技巧
　★ 能擷取大意與關鍵細節
　★ 能根據隱含的線索推論
　★ 能綜合相關資訊預測可能的發展
　★ 能分析、歸納多項訊息的共通點或結論
　★ 能分析判斷文章內容，了解敘述者的觀點、態度及寫作目的

考前提醒

這部份評量考生是否能善用各種閱讀策略，展現出不同層次的閱讀理解能力。作答時需掌握文章的主旨、大意、關鍵細節，了解字裡行間隱含的意義，闡釋作者未於文中直接寫出之訊息，並推測作者的言外之意、觀點和態度。

這個部份的文章形式有說明文、敘述文、論說文等，體裁則包含文章、電子郵件、信件、說明書、報章雜誌、商業文件、圖表、網站資訊等。平時須多接觸各類文體與各式主題文章。

作答時，你可以

1. 先看題目，再閱讀文章

   閱讀文章前先很快地看一次題目，了解題目問什麼或先查看題目出現哪些重要字詞，這麼做能夠引導接下來閱讀的方向，更容易察覺哪些文句可能是答題重點。

2. 找出主題句與關鍵字

   主題句為一個段落的重點所在，概略地說明這段內容的主旨。關鍵字詞則是串聯段落之間的文意。找出主題句與關鍵字幫助我們掌握文章的主旨和核心論點（例如第 23、26、35 題）。圖表題則要看懂標題、縱軸與橫軸中符號所代表的意思，便能掌握圖表的主題（例如第 21-22 題）。

3. 判斷主題句與支持句之間的關聯

   找到主題句與支持句，判斷兩者間的邏輯關係，例如支持句補充說明主題句的論點、舉例呼應主旨、或是提供更詳細的描述等，可以加強對文章的理解（例如第 24、27、29、36、40 題）。

4. 視需要彈性調整閱讀策略

   當有不同的閱讀目的時，要彈性調整閱讀策略。如果只須得到大概的印象，可以略讀文章每個段落的主題句；若是需要掌握細節或是了解所有資訊，則需要精讀，逐字閱讀某些句子或段落。

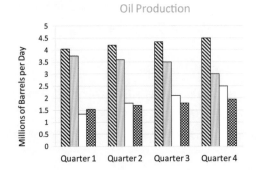

本圖表顯示四個產油國（伊朗、墨西哥、伊拉克、巴西）從第一季到第四季每日石油產量之比較。

What information about the four countries can be learned from the chart?

A. The ratio of their daily oil output to global oil production

B. The amount of oil imported daily from four countries

C. The increase in their daily oil consumption over four quarters

D. The average daily oil output over four quarters

從這個圖表中可以了解到關於這四個國家的什麼資訊？

A. 它們的每日石油產量與全球產量的比例

B. 每日從這四個國家進口的石油量

C. 它們在這四季中每日增加的石油消耗量

D. 它們在這四季中每日平均的石油產量

正解 D

本題問這個圖表顯示了關於這四個國家的什麼資訊，須運用整合圖表資訊並擷取大意的能力。

從圖表標題：oil production（石油產量），縱軸 millions of barrels per day（每日幾百萬桶）及橫軸 quarters 1-4（第 1 至 4 季），可得知此圖表顯示這四個國家第一季到第四季每日石油產量之比較，因此正確答案為 D。

關鍵字詞 output 產量

第 22 題

Which of the following statements is true based on the chart?

A. In the second quarter, oil production in Mexico was half of that in Iraq.

B. In the third quarter, oil production in all of the countries except Iran rose.

C. Oil production in Iraq surpassed that in Brazil in three of the quarters.

D. Oil production in Iran and Mexico rocketed dramatically in the fourth quarter.

根據這個圖表，下列哪一個選項是正確的？

A. 在第二季，墨西哥的石油產量是伊拉克的一半。

B. 在第三季，除了伊朗之外，每一個國家的石油產量都增加。

C. 在四季中有三季伊拉克的石油產量都超過巴西。

D. 在第四季伊朗跟墨西哥的石油產量迅速大幅上升。

正解 C

本題須運用歸納圖表資訊的能力，分析圖表中呈現的趨勢。

作答時，可先閱讀選項，並對照圖表，再一一排除與圖表資訊不符的選項。

選項 A：在第二季，墨西哥的產量是伊拉克的兩倍，非一半。

選項 B：在第三季，除了墨西哥之外，其他國家（包含伊朗）的產量都增加。

選項 C：在四季中有三季伊拉克的產量都超過巴西，因此正解為 C。

選項 D：在第四季，伊朗的產量小幅上漲，但墨西哥的產量下跌，並非兩國的產量都上升。

關鍵字詞　surpass 超過　rocket 迅速上升

接著我們來複習本部份的重點詞彙

output **名** 產量（第 21 題）

例句 • The value of Japan's manufacturing output increased by 2% in June.
六月份日本製造業產值增加百分之二。

surpass **動** 超過（第 22 題）

例句 • Oil production in Iraq surpassed that in Brazil in three of the quarters.
在四季中有三季伊拉克的石油產量都超過巴西。

• The number of Instagram users has surpassed that of Facebook because people like the former's stricter privacy policies.
Instagram 使用人數超越 Facebook，因為人們喜歡前者較嚴謹的隱私政策。

rocket **動** 迅速上升（第 22 題）

例句 • Oil production in Iran and Mexico rocketed dramatically in the fourth quarter.
在第四季伊朗跟墨西哥的石油產量迅速大幅上升。

• Because the summer holidays started, the box office rocketed up 30% from two weeks ago.
因為暑假開始，兩週前電影票房開始飆升百分之三十。

Note

In the 1950s, an English bird lover named Sir Peter Scott introduced ruddy ducks from the U.S. into Britain. A small number of them escaped and bred in the wild. By the early 1990s, they had spread to Spain, arousing fears that they could threaten another duck species.

After ruddy ducks had established themselves in Spain, a hybrid duck species emerged. This came about because ruddy ducks mated not only with their own species, but also with other closely-related ducks. One of these was the white-headed duck, an endangered species in Europe. Given the ruddy duck's aggressive mating behavior, there are concerns that the hybrid species could eventually replace white-headed ducks completely. This has been seen in New Zealand where the introduction of mallards resulted in the catastrophic decline of the native grey duck due to hybridization.

Since 2000, the British government has begun destroying all of the approximately 6,000 ruddy ducks in Britain. Spain followed suit soon afterwards. While the officials admit that this step is regrettable, they maintain that it is the only way to ensure the survival of the white-headed ducks. Meanwhile, opponents of the measure assert that the main danger to white-headed ducks is not breeding with ruddy ducks. Excessive hunting and destruction of their native habitat in Spain are more serious threats. They also call it unacceptable to eliminate one bird species in order to save another.

第 23 題

What is the main subject of this article?

| 這篇文章的主旨為何？

A. Opposition to international trading of birds

B. The potential harm of importing a bird species

C. The evolution of various ducks in Europe

D. Differences between ruddy and white-headed ducks

A. 針對國際間販售鳥類的反對聲浪

B. 進口外來鳥類可能造成的傷害

C. 歐洲地區各種鴨禽類的演化

D. 棕硬尾鴨與白頭鴨的不同之處

正解 Ⓑ

題目問文章的主旨。先略讀找出每個段落的主旨句（請看文章標示紅色的句子），再找出與主旨有關的關鍵字，最後運用整合歸納多項訊息的能力，選出最適合這篇文章的主旨。

第一段提到棕硬尾鴨（ruddy ducks）在英國的起源。第二段接續講述棕硬尾鴨所誕下的混血鴨品種以及牠們造成的生態危機，endangered、aggressive、replace 都是關鍵字。最後一段則以英國大舉撲殺棕硬尾鴨的政策開始，關鍵字詞包括 regrettable、excessive hunting、destruction of habitat 等。整合這些資訊，可以合理判斷正確答案應為 B：The potential harm of importing a bird species（進口外來鳥類可能造成的傷害）。

關鍵字詞 hybrid 混血的 emerge 出現 excessive 過度的 habitat 棲息地 potential 潛在的

Why are New Zealand's mallards and grey ducks mentioned in the second paragraph?

A. To imply that a parallel scenario may happen in Europe

B. To prove that migratory birds are declining on a global scale

C. To compare the behavior of the birds in New Zealand and Britain

D. To draw attention to conservation efforts in New Zealand

文章第二段中為何提到紐西蘭的綠頭鴨與灰鴨?

A. 為了暗示類似情況可能會在歐洲發生

B. 為了證明全球候鳥數量大幅減少

C. 為了比較紐西蘭與英國的鳥類行為

D. 為了將焦點聚集在紐西蘭的保育工作

正解 Ⓐ

本題問作者在文章第二段最後提到紐西蘭的綠頭鴨與灰鴨的用意為何。這個問題與文章的論述結構有關,需要運用根據文本脈絡進行評論與詮釋的能力,判斷主旨與支持句的邏輯關係找出正確答案。

第二段主題句 After ruddy ducks had established themselves in Spain, a **hybrid** duck species emerged. (棕硬尾鴨在西班牙落地生根後,出現了新品種的鴨子),對應第二段最後一句 This has been seen in New Zealand where the introduction of mallards resulted in the catastrophic decline of the native grey duck due to **hybridization**. (紐西蘭曾經發生過這樣的事情,引進外來物種綠頭鴨產生混血品種,以致原生的灰鴨數量災難般地遽減),我們因此建立「混血品種」與「原生品種數量銳減」間的因果關係,可推論曾在紐西蘭發生的事也有可能會在歐洲發生,故正確答案應為 A:To imply that a parallel scenario may happen in Europe(為了暗示類似情況可能會在歐洲發生)。

關鍵字詞 catastrophic 災難的 parallel 類似的、平行 scenario 局面、情節

第 25 題

According to the article, what do the opponents of the government's policy believe?

A. The breeding of ruddy ducks in Spain must be stopped.

B. Both ruddy and white-headed ducks should be preserved.

C. White-headed ducks are an exotic species from the U.S.

D. Ruddy and white-headed ducks are genetically identical.

根據文章，反對政府政策的群眾相信什麼？

A. 必須阻止棕硬尾鴨在西班牙的繁殖。

B. 棕硬尾鴨與白頭鴨皆應受到保育。

C. 白頭鴨是來自美國的外來種。

D. 棕硬尾鴨與白頭鴨是基因相同的物種。

正解 B

題目問的是 What do the opponents of the government's policy believe?（反對政府政策的群眾相信什麼？）。文章中只有第三段提到反對者的立場，因此答案在文章的第三段中。需要運用根據文本脈絡進行評論與詮釋的能力，才能推知正答。

作者認為對白頭鴨而言，大量獵殺與棲息地遭到破壞（excessive hunting and destruction of their native habitat）才是造成生態危機的主因。反對者們認為不應該為了保護一個品種而濫殺另一個品種（unacceptable to eliminate one bird species in order to save another），由此可知正確答案應為 B。

關鍵字詞 eliminate 消滅　preserve 保育

這篇文章為一篇說明文，全文分為三個大段落。主要是關於棕硬尾鴨（ruddy ducks）在歐洲的起源、後續引發的生態危機及社會議論。

段落	主旨	內容
1	棕硬尾鴨（ruddy ducks）在英的起源與牠們所引發的生態危機	棕硬尾鴨在 1950 年代從美國引進至英國。隨後少數在野外繁衍，更在 1990 年代早期擴展至西班牙，引發品種生態危機。
2	棕硬尾鴨造成的生態危機	1. 棕硬尾鴨可與其他相近物種交配，產下的新品種鴨影響歐洲原生物種白頭鴨（white-headed ducks）的生存。 2. 過去在紐西蘭曾有類似的例子，因為外來物種綠頭鴨（mallards）入侵，導致原生物種灰鴨（grey ducks）大量減少。
3	各國政府採取的解決方案與反對者的立場	1. 為保護本土物種的生存，英國與西班牙政府相繼撲殺棕硬尾鴨。 2. 反對政府的聲浪認為造成白頭鴨滅絕的原因是大量獵殺與棲息處遭到破壞。

關鍵字詞

接著我們來複習本部份的重點詞彙

hybrid 形 混血的（第 23 題）

例句
- After ruddy ducks had established themselves in Spain, a hybrid duck species emerged.
  自從棕硬尾鴨在西班牙落地生根後，當地出現了一種新的混血鴨種。

- In nature, hybrid plants are more common than hybrid animals.
  在自然界中，混種植物比混種動物更常見。

emerge 動 出現（第 23 題）

例句
- After days of heavy rain, the sun finally emerged from behind the clouds.
  經過連日大雨，太陽總算撥雲露面了。

excessive 形 過度的（第 23 題）

例句
- Excessive hunting and destruction of their native habitat in Spain are more serious threats to white-headed ducks.
  對白頭鴨而言，大量獵殺與棲息地遭到破壞才是更嚴重的威脅。

- Excessive exercise can sometimes cause serious health problems.
  過度運動有時會造成嚴重的健康問題。

habitat 名 棲息地（第 23 題）

例句
- Climate change is damaging the natural habitat of polar bears in the Arctic Circle.
  氣候變化正在嚴重破壞北極熊位於北極圈的自然棲息地。

potential 形 潛在的（第 23 題）

例句
- Digital marketing helps sellers reach potential buyers from around the world.
  數位行銷幫助賣方與世界各處的潛在買家接洽。

catastrophic 形 災難的（第 24 題）

例句
- The introduction of mallards to New Zealand resulted in the catastrophic decline of the native grey duck due to hybridization.
紐西蘭引進外來物種綠頭鴨產生混血品種，以致原生的灰鴨數量災難般地遽減。

- Despite its quick passage, the hurricane still inflicted catastrophic damage on the city.
即便只是短暫通過，這次的颶風仍對市內造成災難般的損害。

parallel 形 類似的、平行（第 24 題）

例句
- Mary and her mother lived parallel lives, both working as a teacher for more than 40 years before retiring.
Mary 與他母親的人生經歷很相似，兩人都教書超過 40 年才退休。

延伸學習 parallel lines 平行線 parallel universe 平行宇宙

scenario 名 局面、情節（第 24 題）

例句
- Even in a best case scenario, Grandma may still need a wheelchair for a year.
即便在最好的情況下，奶奶還是有可能需要坐輪椅一年。

延伸學習 worst case scenario 最糟糕的情況

eliminate 動 消滅、消除（第 25 題）

例句
- The preservationists call it unacceptable to eliminate one bird species in order to save another.
動物保育人士們認為為了保護一個鳥類品種而消滅另一個品種令人無法接受。

- To avoid allergies, Tina has to eliminate peanuts from her diet.
為了避免過敏，Tina 必須從飲食中剔除花生。

preserve 動 保育（第 25 題）

例句
- The nation is working to preserve its endangered animals.
這個國家正努力保育瀕臨絕種的動物。

延伸思考

讀完文章後，試著回答以下這幾個問題，幫助我們加深對這個議題的了解、啟發更多思考。

1. Do you agree with the policy of eliminating ruddy ducks to preserve a local species as the British and Spanish governments have done?
   你認同英國與西班牙政府採取的撲殺棕硬尾鴨政策嗎？

2. Do you think hunting is destroying the ecological balance?
   你認為打獵是否會破壞自然界的生態平衡？

3. What are some endangered species in Taiwan? What kind of policy is administered to protect them?
   臺灣有哪些瀕臨絕種的本土物種？政府是否有實施什麼保育政策？

Note

While the developed world is suffering from an economic downturn, India is undergoing a period of economic progress similar to that experienced by China over the last thirty years. Analysts forecast that in three years' time, the South Asian giant will post annual GDP growth of 8%, outpacing China's 6%.

Economic reforms enacted during the 1990s are one reason for this surge. India's import tariffs were slashed, and constraints on the entry of foreign firms into Indian markets were removed. Domestic enterprises now operate in a more competitive setting, and they have shown they are ready for the challenge. India's low labor costs and high education level are also working in its favor.

Perhaps the most important factor in India's rise is the composition of its population. In ten years, the number of Indians between the ages of 15 and 64 is expected to exceed one billion. In China, however, this segment of the population will drop by 21 million to 984.4 million. In addition, the number of Indians living in towns and cities should reach 600 million in twenty years, more than double the 290 million measured in the census conducted less than two decades ago. These city dwellers will provide labor for industry and push demand for consumer products.

Pessimists warn that India must tackle certain issues if its growth is to be sustained. The nation's rail network is inadequate, and power outages occur almost daily. Despite these urgent problems, most observers expect India to transform itself in the coming decades.

第 26 題

What is this article mainly about?	這篇文章主要關於什麼？
A. Current social class inequality in India	A. 印度目前不平等的社會階級
B. The crisis of India's population explosion	B. 印度人口爆炸的危機
C. India's ambition to lift average living standards	C. 印度企圖提升平均生活水準的野心
D. An analysis of India's economic prospects	D. 印度經濟前景的分析

正解 Ⓓ

本題問此篇文章的主旨。作答時，先瀏覽各段落的主題句（請看文章標示紅色的句子），再找出關鍵字，例如：progress、surge、composition 等，運用整合歸納多項訊息的能力快速地掌握各段的主要論點。

第一段說明印度的經濟大有起色（undergoing a period of economic progress），第二段說明在 90 年代施行的經濟改革對印度的經濟大有幫助（Economic reforms enacted during the 1990s are one reason for this surge.），第三段說明印度的人口組成對其經濟亦有益處（Perhaps the most important factor in India's rise is the composition of its population.），第四段說明若印度要讓經濟持續發展，有些基本問題須先解決（Pessimists warn that India must tackle certain issues if its growth is to be sustained.）。整合以上資訊後，便可了解作者認為印度經濟雖大有起色，但仍有問題要克服，所以本文主旨為印度經濟前景的分析，因此正確答案為 D。

關鍵字詞　surge 遽增　composition 組成　sustain 保持、維持

According to the article, what change took place in India during the 1990s?

A. Restraints on overseas enterprises were loosened.

B. Large firms expanded their market share.

C. Local investors were compensated for their losses.

D. Manufacturing exports were halted temporarily.

印度在 90 年代發生了什麼改變？

A. 對外國企業的限制鬆綁了。

B. 大公司提升其市場佔有率。

C. 國內投資者獲得其投資失利的賠償。

D. 製造業暫時停止出口。

正解 Ⓐ

本題問印度在 90 年代發生了什麼改變。文章中第二段的主題句明確提到 1990s，因此我們可以得知答案就在第二段，只要仔細閱讀後找出關鍵字，理解文章的字面意義後便可作答。

第二段的主題句為 Economic reforms enacted during the 1990s are one reason for this surge.（在 90 年代施行的經濟改革對印度的經濟大有幫助），接著作者提到兩個經濟改革的措施，包括 India's import tariffs were slashed（進口關稅減少）及 constraints on the entry of foreign firms into Indian markets were removed（外國企業進入印度的限制取消了）。選項 A 提到第二項改革「對外國企業的限制鬆綁了」，且當中的 restraint 為 constraint 同義字，foreign firms 與 overseas enterprises 意思相同，removed 與 loosened 語意相近，因此正確答案為 A。

關鍵字詞 constraint 限制 restraint 抑制 loosen (使) 鬆開

第 28 題

What can be inferred about India's population from this article?

A. The average age has been falling steadily.

B. Households in rural regions are struggling with poverty.

C. It will concentrate further in metropolitan areas.

D. Its rapid increase is a result of mass immigration.

從本文可以推測出關於印度人口的什麼資訊？

A. 平均年齡穩定下降。

B. 在郊區的住戶受貧窮所苦。

C. 未來人口會集中在都會區。

D. 大量移民導致人口快速成長。

正解　Ⓒ

本題問可從本文推測出關於印度人口的什麼資訊。文章中第三段的主題句明確提到人口（population），因此我們可以得知答案就在第三段，接下來仔細閱讀，掌握關鍵訊息，釐清上下文關係並根據語境推敲含意，便可作答。

在第三段中，關於印度人口作者提到兩點：一是年齡集中在 15 到 64 歲，與選項 A 中所提平均年齡下降不符；二是 20 年後，會有約六億人居住在城市，而 20 年前只有約 2.9 億人（In addition, the number of Indians living in towns and cities should reach 600 million in twenty years, more than double the 290 million measured in the census conducted less than two decades ago.），顯示未來人口會集中在都會區，因此正確答案為 C。

關鍵字詞　concentrate 集中　metropolitan 大都市的

How does the writer conclude this article?

A. By giving advice on the control of the birth rate

B. By pressing India's leaders to upgrade health care

C. By stressing the importance of curbing extra spending

D. By pointing out the defects of India's infrastructure

作者如何總結這篇文章？

A. 就控制人口出生率給予忠告

B. 呼籲印度的領導者提升醫療照護

C. 強調減少額外支出的重要性

D. 指出印度基礎建設的缺失

正解 Ⓓ

本題問作者如何總結這篇文章，需要運用釐清上下文關係並根據語境推敲含意的能力。首先，閱讀最後一段的主題句，找到支持句後，釐清兩者間的邏輯關係，便可作答。

從最後一段的主題句 Pessimists warn that India must tackle certain issues if its growth is to be sustained. 可以得知雖然印度經濟的前景看來非常樂觀，但仍有一些問題需要解決。支持這個論點的句子接著補充是哪些問題需要解決：The nation's rail network is inadequate, and power outages occur almost daily.（鐵路系統不足，跳電更是家常便飯。）此處的 rail network 及 power 正是 infrastructure 的一部份，因此正確答案為 D。

關鍵字詞 infrastructure 基礎建設 defect 缺陷 inadequate 不足的 outage 停電期間

📋 文本分析

這篇文章為一篇說明文，全文分為四個大段落。主要是關於印度的經濟前景。

段落	主旨	內容
1	印度的經濟大有起色	專家預測印度的 GDP 成長將超越中國。
2	在 90 年代施行的經濟改革對印度帶來益處	1. 對外國企業更友善，例如降低關稅及鬆綁限制。 2. 本國企業準備好面臨更具競爭力的市場。 3. 勞工成本低廉但教育程度高更是一大優勢。
3	印度的人口移居城市對其經濟亦有助益	1. 人口將集中在 15 到 64 歲。 2. 都市人口將大幅成長。
4	印度基礎建設的問題必須解決	1. 鐵路系統不足。 2. 常跳電。

關鍵字詞

接著我們來複習本部份的重點詞彙

surge 名 遽增（第 26 題）

例句 • Economic reforms enacted during the 1990s are one reason for the surge in their annual GDP.
1990 年代所施行的經濟改革是他們年度國內生產總額驟升的原因之一。

• After a cup of strong black coffee, Janice felt a surge of energy as she went back into the meeting.
喝了一杯濃烈的黑咖啡後，Janice 充滿精力地返回會議。

composition 名 組成（第 26 題）

例句 • One of the most important factors in India's rise is the composition of its population.
印度崛起的一個重要因素之一是它的人口組成。

• Nowadays, numerous artificial ingredients are added to cosmetics so the composition of cosmetics is strictly regulated.
現今許多化妝品中都有添加人工原料，因此化妝品成分被嚴格控管。

sustain 動 保持、維持（第 26 題）

例句 • Pessimists warn that India must tackle certain issues if its growth is to be sustained.
保守人士認為若印度想維持其發展，必須要解決一些問題。

• To conserve endangered species helps sustain the diversity of life.
保育瀕臨滅絕的物種有助維持生物多樣性。

constraint 名 限制（第 27 題）

例句
- India's import tariffs were slashed, and constraints on the entry of foreign firms into Indian markets were removed.
  印度進口關稅減少，且外國企業進入印度的限制也被取消了。

- Constraints on distance learning include the difficulty of receiving immediate feedback and the lack of peer interaction.
  遠距學習的限制包括難以得到即時反饋和缺乏同儕互動。

restraint 名 抑制（第 27 題）

例句
- The court imposed restraints on freedom of the press so that the trial would not be affected by publicity.
  法庭限制新聞自由，以確保審判不受社會輿論影響。

loosen 動 （使）鬆開（第 27 題）

例句
- The jelly jar was sealed tight so the child asked his father to loosen the lid.
  果醬瓶密封得緊，因此小孩請他父親打開瓶蓋。

concentrate 動 集中（第 28 題）

例句
- Children who consume too much sugar may have problems concentrating in class.
  攝取太多糖份的小孩可能難以集中注意力學習。

metropolitan 形 大都市的（第 28 題）

例句
- Dynamic economic activities happen in metropolitan areas so there are more job opportunities.
  都會區的商業活動非常活躍，因此有較多就業機會。

infrastructure 名 基礎建設（第 29 題）

例句
- During the war, much of the region's infrastructure, namely bridges, railways and power plants, was destroyed.
  戰爭時期，許多基礎建設遭到毀壞，像是橋、鐵路和發電廠。

defect 名 缺陷（第 29 題）

例句 • The ticket booking website collapsed so the engineer had to correct a defect in the program.
訂票網站當機，因此工程師必須修正程式錯誤。

inadequate 形 不足的（第 29 題）

例句 • The nation's rail network is inadequate, and power outages occur almost daily.
這個國家的鐵路網絡還不足夠，且停電幾乎是天天發生。

• After the typhoon, the village suffered from an inadequate food supply so the government called for donations from the public.
颱風之後，這個村落飽受食物匱乏之苦，因此政府向社會大眾募捐。

outage 名 停電期間（第 29 題）

例句 • Because of a sudden power outage, my laptop shut down, and I failed to recover the paragraphs that I had yet to save.
因為突然停電，我的筆電斷電，我找不回剛剛還沒儲存的段落。

延伸思考

讀完文章後，試著回答以下這幾個問題，幫助我們加深對這個議題的了解、啟發更多思考。

1. Have you ever been to India? What are the similarities and differences between India described in this article and your image of the place prior to reading this article?
   你是否去過印度？文章中的印度與你所知的印度有什麼異同之處？

2. What are the possible changes a society may go through when its economy is rapidly growing?
   當一個國家經濟快速發展，社會可能會經歷什麼改變呢？

3. Does the political instability of a country affect its economic development?
   一個國家的政治不穩定是否會影響其經濟發展？

Note

Questions 30-34 are based on the information provided in the following web page and email.

www.icmss.org.tw/conference

The Fifth International Conference on Management and Social Sciences (ICMSS)
Call for Papers

The ICMSS, now in its fifth year, is a platform for scholars to discuss research in the fields of Communication & Society, Politics & Law, Banking & Finance, and Marketing & Management.

The Fifth ICMSS will take place in Taipei, Taiwan. Researchers at universities, colleges or research institutes are invited to submit original papers to the following email account: papers@icmss.org.tw. Only upon payment of the registration fee (US$110) will submissions be reviewed for inclusion at this year's conference. All submissions will be peer reviewed by three competent referees. Authors of accepted papers may be required to amend their work as advised by the review panel. Revised papers must be submitted by the deadline below.

Important dates

Deadline for paper submission: July 1
Notification of acceptance: August 20
Deadline for submission of revised paper: September 20
Conference dates: November 10-12

Notes

For format guidelines, please click here. Papers that do not conform to the requirements will be returned for modification.

If you have questions, please write to Judy Hall at jh@icmss.org.tw.

From: Dennis Burton <dburton@univmail.edu>

To: Judy Hall <jh@icmss.org.tw>

Subject: Questions about the 5th ICMSS

Dear Ms. Hall,

Thank you for your prompt response. I have paid the registration fee as per your instructions. However, in my previous email, I also asked whether submission of multiple articles is accepted. I hope you can clarify this as soon as possible. Both articles I plan to submit are co-authored with my colleague Professor R. Jones. Although the papers both concern the role of central banks in managing the money supply, they are written from different perspectives. I believe that they will be of great interest to the target audience of this conference.

In addition, there still appears to be a problem with the link on the website. I have tried the web browser you suggested, but I still received a "Cannot find expected page" notification.

Thank you for your assistance. I look forward to hearing from you.

Best regards,
Dennis Burton

這個閱讀題組共包含兩篇文章，一篇是網頁上的活動介紹，另一篇是電子郵件。網頁的活動介紹文主要為一研討會的徵稿公告及相關資訊，電子郵件的內容則是一位有意投稿者向主辦單位詢問問題。

What is the main purpose of the notice?

此公告的目的為何?

A. To announce a chance to win a valuable scholarship

A. 宣布一個贏得高額獎學金的機會

B. To welcome conference participants to a banquet

B. 歡迎研討會與會者參加晚宴

C. To seek contributions to an academic event

C. 替一個學術活動徵稿

D. To specify the theme of an annual seminar

D. 明確指出一個年度研討會的主題

正解 C

本題問的是這個公告的目的。先瀏覽公告的標題,尋找關鍵字(以紅字標示),整合歸納多項訊息,便能判斷公告的主旨。

標題中的 conference(會議)及 call for papers(誠徵論文),表示這是一個學術活動在徵稿,也就是這個公告的目的,因此正確答案為 C。

關鍵字詞 academic 學術的 contribution 貢獻、投稿

第 31 題

What might some researchers receive on August 20?

A. Invitations to give speeches to undergraduate students

B. Suggestions to enhance the quality of manuscripts

C. Cash rewards for assisting in the preparation of a meeting

D. Reminders about equipment that will be provided

研究者在八月二十日可能會收到什麼？

A. 對大學生演講的邀請

B. 加強稿件品質的建議

C. 協助會議籌備的現金獎勵

D. 關於可提供的設備之提醒

 正解 Ⓑ

本題問研究者在八月二十日可能會收到什麼。答案應該在網頁內容的細部資訊中，所以先找出哪一個段落提到八月二十日，再閱讀上下文，判斷它們的因果或邏輯關係。

首先，八月二十日出現在 **Important dates** 下的 Notification of acceptance: August 20，表示投稿者會在八月二十日收到稿件是否被接受的通知，但是題目不是問這個，所以我們繼續閱讀上下文，就會發現上一段提到 Authors of accepted papers may be required to amend their work as advised by the review panel. 表示被接受的稿件必須要根據提供的修改建議修改後再寄一次，而提供修改建議的目的正是改善稿件的品質，因此正確答案為 **B**。

關鍵字詞 notification 通知　amend 修改　enhance 加強　manuscript 原稿

第 32 題

When did Dennis write the email?

A. Before July 1

B. On August 20

C. In mid September

D. After November 12

Dennis 是什麼時候寫這封電子郵件？

A. 七月一日前

B. 八月二十日

C. 九月中

D. 十一月十二日後

正解 Ⓐ

本題問 Dennis 是什麼時候寫這封電子郵件。電子郵件中 Dennis 未提到明確的日期，所以必須整合歸納多篇文本中的訊息，先從電子郵件中的其他線索，再對照網頁公告上的日期來推論。

Dennis 在電子郵件中詢問同一個作者是否能投多篇論文，接著提到他想投兩篇，而且兩篇都是他跟他同事寫的（Both articles I plan to submit are co-authored with my colleague Professor R. Jones.），此處的 plan to 表示他尚未完成投稿這個動作。接著對照網頁公告，可知投稿的截止日為七月一日（Deadline for paper submission: July 1），表示 Dennis 是在投稿截止日前寫這封電子郵件，因此正確答案為 A。

關鍵字詞 submission 呈遞 deadline 截止日

第 33 題

What can be inferred about Dennis?

A. His initial inquiries were fully answered.

B. His colleague introduced Ms. Hall to him.

C. He has yet to complete a course of study.

D. He has written two articles on similar topics.

我們可以推論出關於 Dennis 的什麼事？

A. 他先前的詢問已全部獲得回覆。

B. 他的同事介紹 Ms. Hall 給他。

C. 他還沒修習完畢一門課。

D. 他寫了兩篇主題類似的文章。

正解 D

本題問我們可以推論出關於 Dennis 的什麼事。答案應該是在 Dennis 的電子郵件中，先瀏覽郵件中兩個段落的主旨句，確定在哪一個段落後，再根據語境推敲含意。

Dennis 的電子郵件第一段提到他先前已寫信給 Ms. Hall，詢問同一個作者可否同時投遞兩份稿，但 Ms. Hall 沒有回答他的問題，所以他希望這次 Ms. Hall 能夠給他清楚的答覆。第二段則是有關網頁問題，與四個選項皆無關聯。回到第一段，他提到自己繳交了兩篇論文，雖然主題類似，但是分別以不同的角度討論（Although the papers both concern the role of central banks in managing the money supply, they are written from different perspectives.）。由此可知，Dennis 寫了兩篇主題類似的文章，正確答案為 D。

關鍵字詞 inquiry 詢問

Which feature of the ICMSS website does Dennis report as NOT functioning as expected?

A. One that enables applicants to pay a fee

B. One that describes key committee members

C. One that refers to standards to be followed

D. One that outlines the process of registration

Dennis 通報 ICMSS 網站的哪一個功能無法正常運作？

A. 能讓申請者付費的功能

B. 能描述委員會重要成員的功能

C. 能提供應遵循之標準的功能

D. 能大略說明註冊流程的功能

正解 C

本題問 Dennis 通報 ICMSS 網站的哪一個功能無法正常運作。整合歸納文本中的訊息發現，Dennis 的電子郵件中只提到網站的連結有問題，沒有提到這個連結的功能，所以必須回到網頁公告找答案。

在網頁公告中，只有 Notes 下面才有提供 link（連結），所以答案就在這一段。而這個 link 是提供稿件格式，給有意投稿的人參考（For format guidelines, please click here.），而 guidelines（準則）就是 standards（標準、準則），因此正確答案為 C。

關鍵字詞 format 格式 guideline 準則

🔍 關鍵字詞

接著我們來複習本部份的重點詞彙

academic 形 學術的（第 30 題）

例句 • A student's academic performance is influenced by several factors like motivations and learning styles.
一位學生的學術表現受數種因素影響，例如：動機和學習風格。

contribution 名 貢獻、投稿（第 30 題）

• The doctor accepted a prestigious award for his lifetime contribution to public health in rural communities.
這位醫生因為終生奉獻於鄉村社區的公共衛生而獲頒殊榮。

notification 名 通知（第 31 題）

例句 • Upon receiving the notification, a student learns the result of the housing application.
一收到通知，學生就能得知住宿申請的結果。

amend 動 修改（第 31 題）

例句 • Authors of accepted papers may be required to amend their work as advised by the review panel.
入選的論文作者可能須依照評審委員提供之建議修改其論文內容。

• Since laws and treaties are occasionally amended, lawyers need to keep up to date with these revisions.
因為法規條文有時會修改，律師需跟進這些最新修訂。

enhance 動 加強（第 31 題）

例句 • With an increase of 10 percent in annual fee to the trade union, benefits of membership were enhanced, for example, more rent subsidies.
工會的年費增加百分之十，會員權益獲得改善，例如更多的租金補助。

manuscript 名 原稿（第 31 題）

例句 • Instead of delivering a manuscript to publishers by hand or through the mail, authors nowadays usually send their drafts via electronic files.
有別於以往親送或寄送手稿到出版社，現今作家通常是透過電子檔傳送。

submission 名 呈遞（第 32 題）

例句 • Only upon payment of the registration fee (US$110) will submissions be reviewed for inclusion at this year's conference.
繳交註冊費（美金 110 元）後，您的稿件才會進入今年研討會的審稿階段。

• If a submission is successful, the email system will reply automatically.
若資料繳交成功，電子郵件系統會自動回覆。

deadline 名 截止日（第 32 題）

例句 • Revised papers must be submitted by the deadline below.
修改過的論文須於下列的截止期限內繳交。

• I need to submit the abstract before the deadline; otherwise, my application will be rejected.
我必須在截止日前繳交摘要，否則我的申請將會被拒。

inquiry 名 詢問（第 33 題）

例句 • The flight attendant was tired of the child's constant inquiries so she gave him a stern look.
空服員對小孩不斷的詢問感到厭煩，所以她向他嚴厲一瞥。

format 名 格式（第 34 題）

例句 • For format guidelines, please click here.
如需稿件格式準則，請按此處。

• The format of a journal paper is fixed, so authors cannot randomly adjust the font size and margins.
期刊文章的格式是固定的，所以作者不能隨意調整字體大小和邊界。

guideline　名　準則（第 34 題）

例句　• To request a tax refund, tourists follow a guideline for completing the procedure.
旅客按照準則來完成申報退稅的手續。

Note

Studies have shown that the earth is warming as a consequence of carbon emissions. Carbon dioxide (CO_2) is released when power is generated by burning fossil fuels, such as coal, oil, or natural gas. The rising level of CO_2 in the atmosphere is causing it to retain more energy radiated by the earth. (5) Therefore, the earth's atmosphere is warming, bringing about climatic change.

Some governments are committed to reducing atmospheric warming by reducing carbon emissions. For that to happen, heavy industries must cut their consumption of fossil fuels. Some economists recommend using "cap and trade" to achieve this goal. In this system, each company purchases an (10) official permit, allowing its factories or other facilities to emit CO_2 into the atmosphere. To operate, a large corporation may need to buy thousands of such permits worth millions of dollars. Cap and trade is meant to limit the total CO_2 that is produced. Unfortunately, this method is extremely complicated. It is also expensive for consumers since firms cover the cost of their permits by (15) charging more for their merchandise and services.

An alternative to limiting carbon emissions with fewer detrimental consequences is to adopt the "carbon taxes approach." A carbon tax is either a tax on a specific fossil fuel, such as coal, or a tax on electricity that is generated using fossil fuels. Such a tax convinces both companies and consumers to (20) use less energy from fossil fuels. The more fossil fuels or electricity a firm consumes, the higher the carbon tax it must pay to the government. Thus, energy companies can deduct their carbon taxes by producing electricity using wind or solar power instead of fossil fuels. And other firms can lower their taxes by installing more efficient equipment that uses less electricity.

(25)　　In this approach, carbon taxes are also added to consumers' utility bills. So the more electricity a consumer consumes, the more tax he or she is charged. Like companies, consumers can pay lower carbon taxes by using less electricity. This motivates them to abandon wasteful habits and install energy-efficient appliances and light bulbs in their homes.

(30)　　Carbon taxes do more than just cut consumption of fossil fuels. They also provide capital for environmental and charitable projects. Funds collected through carbon taxes can be used to finance the advancement of "green" products and technologies. Alternatively, <u>they</u> can be employed to fight hunger or disease around the globe. With so many advantages, carbon taxes are clearly a better choice.

What is the main purpose of this article?

A. To identify factors leading to deteriorating air quality

B. To outline a strategy related to tax avoidance

C. To defend a project aimed at restoring household electricity

D. To contrast schemes for discouraging the use of fossil fuels

本文的目的為何？

A. 辨識造成空氣品質惡化的因素

B. 概述避稅的策略

C. 捍衛恢復家庭用電的計畫

D. 對比抑制使用化石燃料的方案

正解 D

本題問本文的目的為何。先瀏覽每個段落的主題句（請看文章標示紅色的句子），再找出與支持句的關係，掌握各段的核心論點後，便可了解全文主旨。

第一段簡單介紹使用化石燃料排放二氧化碳導致全球暖化的背景，第二段開始切入正題，主題句點明各國政府致力於降低二氧化碳排放（Some governments are committed to reducing atmospheric warming by reducing carbon emissions.），後續的支持句說明實際做法，也就是「排汙交易」cap and trade（For that to happen, heavy industries must cut their consumption of fossil fuels. Some economists recommend using "cap and trade" to achieve this goal.）。所以我們了解 cap and trade 是降低二氧化碳排放的方法之一。接下來第三段主題句提到了另一個降低二氧化碳排放的方法，而且比 cap and trade 更好（An alternative to limiting carbon emissions with fewer detrimental consequences is to adopt the "carbon taxes approach."），也就是徵收碳稅。第四段與第五段繼續深入探討此一作法。整合以上資訊可知本文的目的為對比排汙交易及徵收碳稅這兩個方案，它們的目的都是抑制化石燃料的使用，因此正確答案為 D。

關鍵字詞 emission 排放 detrimental 有危害的

第 36 題

What is true about the phenomenon described in the first paragraph?

A. It occurs periodically in nature.

B. Its cause is already understood.

C. It depletes natural resources.

D. Its impact is diminishing.

關於第一段描述的現象何者是正確的？

A. 它定期會自然發生。

B. 它的起因已被了解。

C. 它耗費自然資源。

D. 它的影響變小了。

正解 B

本題問關於第一段描述的現象何者是正確的。閱讀這一段的主題句判斷題目問的現象為何，根據文本脈絡詮釋語意，就能找出正確答案。

從主題句 Studies have shown that the earth is warming as a consequence of carbon emissions. 便可得知題目問的現象為全球暖化，接下來的支持句解釋全球暖化發生的原因，由此可知這個現象發生的原因已為人所知，因此正確答案為 B。

關鍵字詞 atmosphere 大氣層 retain 保留 radiate 輻射、放射

Which of the following disadvantages does the writer indicate about the cap and trade method?

A. It is impractical.

B. It incurs enormous debts.

C. It is strongly biased.

D. It takes time to get a permit.

作者在文章中提出下列哪個排汙交易方案的缺點?

A. 它不切實際。

B. 它會造成巨額的負債。

C. 它太偏頗。

D. 它取得許可太花時間。

正解 A

本題問作者在文章中提出哪一個排汙交易方案的缺點。需要根據文本脈絡進行評論與詮釋,閱讀時利用掃讀(scanning)的技巧找到 cap and trade 的主要說明(第二段),接著快速瀏覽這一段內容並找出較負面的敘述就可作答。

第二段作者總共提到了三個關於 cap and trade 的缺點:

1. 公司必須取得數千個許可,增加成本 (To operate, a large corporation may need to buy thousands of such permits worth millions of dollars.)

2. 正因如此複雜性也變高(this method is extremely complicated)

3. 公司把取得許可的成本轉嫁給消費者,增加消費者的負擔(It is also expensive for consumers since firms cover the cost of their permits by charging more for their merchandise and services.)

整合以上資訊,可以得知 cap and trade 這個作法不切實際,因此正確答案為 A。

關鍵字詞 impractical 不實際的 permit 許可

第 38 題

What does the cap and trade method cause companies to do?

A. Remedy their deficits

B. Raise their retail prices

C. Lay off employees in difficult times

D. Form long-standing partnerships

排汙交易方案促使公司做什麼？

A. 修補赤字

B. 提高零售價格

C. 經營困難時解雇員工

D. 建立長期的夥伴關係

正解 **B**

本題問排汙交易方案促使公司做什麼。排汙交易的說明在第二段，釐清這一段關於公司處理因排汙交易產生的成本之因果關係，並根據語境推敲含意，就可找出正確答案。

在第二段作者說明公司如何因應排汙交易所產生的成本，因果關係如下：

因 Cause	公司必須取得數千個許可，成本增加 （To operate, a large corporation may need to buy thousands of such permits worth millions of dollars.）
果 Effect	公司藉由提高它們產品或服務的價格，把取得許可的成本轉嫁給消費者 （It is also expensive for consumers since firms cover the cost of their permits by charging more for their merchandise and services.）

整合以上資訊，我們可以得知排汙交易促使公司提高零售價格，因此正確答案為 B。

關 鍵 字 詞 retail 零售 merchandise 商品、物品

What does the writer explain about carbon taxes in this article?

A. How they promote the acceptance of renewable energy

B. Why authorities have insisted on modifying this system

C. How they are related to wage earners' income

D. Why their significance is overestimated

關於課徵碳稅作者提出什麼說明？

A. 它們如何提升對於再生能源的接受度

B. 為何執政者堅持修改這個制度

C. 它們與受薪階級人士有何關係

D. 為何它們的重要性被高估了

正解 Ⓐ

本題問關於碳稅方案作者提出什麼說明。首先必須釐清上下文關係，作者在第三段主要說明徵收碳稅對公司的影響，瀏覽該段主題句後，掌握重點論述，鎖定資訊，便可作答。

作者在第三段說明徵收碳稅基本上是一個以價制量的概念，使用燃燒化石燃料產生的能源越多，要繳交的稅額也就越高（The more fossil fuels or electricity a firm consumes, the higher the carbon tax it must pay to the government.）。正因為如此，能源公司為了避免繳交稅款，只好轉向再生能源發電，例如風力或太陽能等（Thus, energy companies can deduct their carbon taxes by producing electricity using wind or solar power instead of fossil fuels.），間接提升了再生能源的接受度，因此正確答案為 A。

關鍵字詞 deduct 減去、扣除

第 40 題

What does "they" in line 33 refer to?	第 33 行的 they 指的是什麼？
A.　Joint ventures	A.　合資企業
B.　Medical facilities	B.　醫療設施
C.　Financial assets	C.　金融資產
D.　Instant cures	D.　即時治療

正解　C

本題問第 33 行的 they 指稱為何。仔細閱讀這個有 they 的句子，接著閱讀上下文，根據語境推敲含意，便可確認答案。

從主題句（Carbon taxes do more than just cut consumption of fossil fuels.）可得知這一段主要談論碳稅的優點。除了降低化石燃料的使用外，徵收的稅款更可用於資助既環保又公益的綠能源產品或科技，更可用來協助打擊飢餓及疾病問題，造福更多人，注意作者用了 alternatively（另一方面）引導出碳稅的另一個用途。

所以第 33 行的 they 指的就是 funds collected through carbon taxes（碳稅徵得的資金），而 financial assets（資產）正包含了 funds（資金），因此正確答案為 C。

關鍵字詞　charitable 慈善的　employ 應用　asset 資產、財產

文本分析

這篇文章為一篇論說文，全文分為五個大段落。主要是比較對抗全球暖化的兩種方法：排汙交易及徵收碳稅。

段落	主旨	內容
1	燃燒化石燃料已被證明會造成全球暖化	燃燒化石燃料會釋放二氧化碳，加劇溫室效應，形成全球暖化。
2	私人企業採取排汙交易的方式來抑制二氧化碳的排放	1. 公司必須購買排放許可供其排放固定數量的二氧化碳。 2. 過程很複雜。 3. 一家公司須購買數千個許可，造成成本增加。 4. 公司將這筆成本轉嫁給消費者，增加消費者負擔。
3	徵收碳稅是另一個抑制二氧化碳排放的方法	1. 碳排放量越高，要繳的碳稅越多。 2. 為避免高額稅款，企業改為使用再生能源或省電裝置。
4	消費者用電越少，要繳的碳稅就越低	消費者為避免高額稅款，改變生活習慣或使用省電家電。
5	徵收碳稅比排汙交易更理想	碳稅所得可用來研發綠能源科技、打擊全球飢餓或疾病問題。

🔍 關鍵字詞

接著我們來複習本部份的重點詞彙

emission 名 排放（第 35 題）

例句
- Studies have shown that the earth is warming as a consequence of carbon emissions.
  研究發現全球暖化起因為二氧化碳的排放。

- Since global warming affects sea levels and temperatures, carbon emissions should be limited as much as possible.
  因為全球暖化影響海平面高度和氣溫，碳排放量應盡可能被限制。

detrimental 形 有危害的（第 35 題）

例句
- An alternative to limiting carbon emissions with fewer detrimental consequences is to adopt the "carbon taxes approach."
  減少碳排放且危害較小的替代方案是採用徵收碳稅，它的負面影響較小。

- While we understand the harm caused by insufficient sleep, excessive sleep is also detrimental to human health.
  我們雖知道睡眠不足所造成的傷害，但過長的睡眠也會危害人體健康。

atmosphere 名 大氣層（第 36 題）

例句
- The rising level of CO_2 in the atmosphere is causing it to retain more energy radiated by the earth.
  大氣層中攀升的二氧化碳濃度導致地球無法散熱。

- Due to the changing air pressure in the atmosphere, chip bags expand as altitude increases.
  由於大氣壓力的改變，洋芋片包裝隨海拔高度增加而膨脹。

retain 動 保留（第 36 題）

例句
- It is suggested that customers retain the receipts from their purchases for a month, especially expensive ones.
  建議顧客保留購物收據一個月，尤其是高價的物品。

radiate 動 輻射、放射（第 36 題）

例句 • The campfire is radiating heat, warming the people sitting around it.
營火散發熱能，溫暖著坐在周圍的人們。

impractical 形 不切實際的（第 37 題）

例句 • It is impractical to solely rely on solar energy owing to the high cost in maintenance of solar panels.
完全仰賴太陽能發電是不切實際的，因為太陽能板的維護成本高。

permit 名 許可（第 37 題）

例句 • Each company purchases an official permit, allowing its factories or other facilities to emit CO_2 into the atmosphere.
每一間公司須購買一個官方許可，允許其工廠或其他設備排放二氧化碳至大氣中。

• Without a permit from the city government, street artists cannot perform in public.
未經市政府許可，街頭藝人不能在公共場所表演。

retail 名 零售（第 38 題）

例句 • Compared to wholesale businesses, retail shops sell products in smaller quantities.
和量販店相比，零售商店販賣較小量的商品。

merchandise 名 商品、物品（第 38 題）

例句 • It is also expensive for consumers since firms cover the cost of their permits by charging more for their merchandise and services.
公司會將購買許可的費用成本轉嫁至商品與服務的價格上，因此對消費者而言也是相當昂貴的。

• The merchandise is displayed in a transparent window, and customers can inquire about the items that they wish to buy.
商品在透明櫥窗展示，顧客可以詢問有意購買的品項。

deduct 動 減去、扣除（第 39 題）

例句 • Companies can deduct their carbon taxes by producing electricity using wind or solar power instead of fossil fuels.
能源公司為了減輕碳稅，只好轉向發展風力或太陽能發電，而非化石燃料。

• Payment for the national health insurance is deducted from an individual's monthly income.
全民健康保險的支付從個人月薪扣除。

charitable 形 慈善的（第 40 題）

例句 • Carbon taxes provide capital for environmental and charitable projects.
碳稅為環境事業和慈善專案提供經費。

• The orphanage mainly depends on charitable donations to cover its expenses.
這所兒童之家主要仰賴慈善捐贈因應支出。

employ 動 應用（第 40 題）

例句 • Funds can be employed to fight hunger or disease around the globe.
資金可用於打擊全球飢餓與疾病問題。

• Rather than searching manually, the researcher employs a sensor to detect rising pollution degrees.
這個研究員應用感應器來偵測汙染上升程度，而非人工搜尋。

asset 名 資產、財產（第 40 題）

例句 • The U.S.-based furniture company reached $1 billion in assets, and will open its first showroom in Asia soon.
這間美國家具公司資產達到十億，近期將會開設亞洲的第一間展銷廳。

讀完文章後，試著回答以下這幾個問題，幫助我們加深對這個議題的了解、啟發更多思考。

1. Do you agree that Taiwan should implement carbon taxes?
   你贊成臺灣開始徵收碳稅嗎？

2. Are people in Taiwan well-informed and educated about climate change? Why or why not?
   你認為臺灣人民是否充分了解氣候變遷？為什麼？

3. Do you agree that the government should actively encourage the development of green energy industries?
   你認為政府是否應更積極鼓勵綠能產業的發展？

Note

學習策略

1. **積極主動探索有興趣的課外文章，擴展學習場域，並規劃執行精讀的六大步驟 SQ4R**

   (1) **Survey**（瀏覽）：先快速瀏覽文章，可以先閱讀每個段落的第一句，如果是一本書，則可先從前言、目錄、圖表、結論和索引開始看起，這麼做可以快速掌握大概內容。

   (2) **Question**（提問）：大略知道文章的內容後，可先利用 **5W1H** 進行提問（who、what、when、where、why and how），再試著問自己一些與主題相關的問題，例如自己對於這個主題已知多少、預測作者討論的內容與態度等，先設想好這些問題可以有更明確的指引，也能有效提高閱讀動機。

   (3) **Read**（閱讀）：用心仔細閱讀文章，留意文章重點以及主要的概念，確保自己完全理解。使用螢光筆標示重要字句，並可在旁留下筆記，方便日後複習。

   (4) **Recite**（覆述）：趁剛讀完文章、印象最深刻的時候，蓋上書本或文章，練習自問自答。自問文章的主旨是什麼、作者提出什麼關鍵細節來佐證論點。回答問題時，可以先試著從文章中找到回答問題的句子，再試著用自己的話回答問題。這麼做可以幫助你練習不同層次的理解能力，培養問題理解、思辨分析、推理批判的系統思考與後設思考素養。

   (5) **Record**（記錄）：試著用自己的話將重點寫下來，包括文章主旨、論點、結論，留下此次閱讀的紀錄。並可以回想自己閱讀前提出的問題，作者是否有如自己預期的提到某些論點、或是否如預期一樣採取某種態度。

   (6) **Review**（複習）：再次回想文章的重點，將不同的段落關係連結起來，讓整篇文章的脈絡更清晰。

2. 透過延伸問題培養獨立思考的習慣

每閱讀完一篇文章，可以就文本的內容練習延伸思考，像是「是否認同作者舉的例子」、「是否認同作者的立場」、「可否舉出相同或相反的例子」。藉由回答這些問題釐清自己的想法與理由，將讀到的資訊連結自身經驗、思想與價值，對文本提出行動與反思批判。這個練習不僅能幫助加深對這個議題的了解、還可以啟發更多思考。

3. 養成主動閱讀英語讀物的習慣，並拓展閱讀的主題與文類

廣泛閱讀不同文類，例如報章新聞、小說類（fiction）以及非小說類（non-fiction）等長篇讀物，熟悉不同體裁的寫作風格與特色，包括商務書信、說明文、敘事文與論說文等，將有助於面對各種新的閱讀情境，運用已習得的英語文知識有效解決問題，展現自我精進、符號運用與溝通表達的核心素養。

4. 練習整合多篇文本的訊息

日常和工作時經常需要針對單一主題多文本閱讀，透過閱讀而學習（read to learn）不同文本建構、統整相關訊息。通過中高級測驗的學習者英語能力逐漸成熟，應用領域擴大，閱讀多篇文本的機會也隨之變多。如何培養整合多篇文本訊息的能力呢？建議學習者平時閱讀時可主動尋找不同文體的文章，試著整合歸納兩篇文本的相同或相異處，並明確指出推論的依據。再者，學習者初次面對多篇閱讀題型時，建議可適時運用略讀、搜尋閱讀等技巧，提升預測問題的準確度，增加閱讀的效率。只要平日閱讀時多練習，你會發現多篇閱讀的題型其實沒那麼難。

學習者平時只要腳踏實地的打好基本功，持續練習，測驗時就能從容應答。

Note

全民英檢學習指南－中高級聽讀測驗

主　　編：沈冬

編 輯 群：財團法人語言訓練測驗中心（LTTC）

出 版 者：財團法人語言訓練測驗中心（LTTC）

地　　址：10663 臺北市大安區辛亥路二段 170 號

電　　話：（02）2362-6385 傳真：（02）2364-0379

網　　址：www.lttc.ntu.edu.tw

封面設計：恣遊設計有限公司

印　　刷：秋雨創新股份有限公司

出版日期：民國 109 年 3 月初版

定　　價：平裝本新臺幣 380 元

ISBN 978-986-94222-4-6 （平裝附光碟片）

全民英檢學習指南 中高級聽讀測驗／沈冬主編 . --

初版 . -- 臺北市：語言訓練測驗中心，民 109.03

　　冊；　公分

ISBN 978-986-94222-4-6（平裝附光碟片）

1. 英語 2. 讀本

805.1892　　　　　　　　　　109000867